RIVALS

A LA RUE FAMILY CRIME THRILLER

RICHARD WAKE

MANOR AND STATE, LLC

SIGN UP FOR MY READING GROUP AND RECEIVE A FREE NOVELLA!

I'd love to have you join my on my writing journey. In addition to receiving my newsletter, which contains news about my upcoming books, you'll also receive a FREE novella. Its title is *Ominous Austria*, and it is a prequel to my first series.

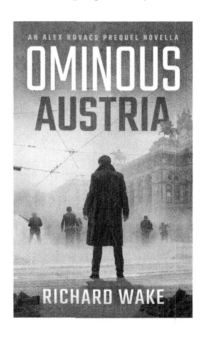

The main character, Alex Kovacs, is an everyman who is presented with an opportunity to make a difference on the eve of the Nazis' takeover of Austria. But what can one man do? It is the question that hangs over the entire series, taking Alex from prewar Austria to the Cold War, from Vienna, to Switzerland, to France, and to Eastern Europe.

To receive *Ominous Austria*, as well as the newsletter, click here:

https://dl.bookfunnel.com/ur7seb8qeg

PART I

1

—————

"So, where's the other one?" Sylvie said. Henri was almost happy she had something to bitch about other than the food, which was one of her greatest hits. Then again, complaining about their daughter was pretty high on the list, too.

"Don't know — she doesn't share her calendar with me," Henri said.

"She should, you know, if she's going to play at this."

"It's not playing, dear. You've seen the envelopes."

"It's a phase."

"A pretty lucrative phase, then — as lucrative for you as for me, in case you hadn't noticed."

"She's a kid," Sylvie said.

"With a degree in finance."

Sylvie waved dismissively. Then she made a noise that was the bastard child of a sigh and a fart. Then she said, "Our kid, and you know our kids."

"You know I'm sitting right here," Guy said. He was Sylvie and Henri's other kid.

"I wasn't sure you could hear, you know, over the clatter of the cutlery," Sylvie said.

Guy was the only one who actually liked the food at Vincent's, the restaurant where the La Rue family always held these gatherings. It was platters of either pork or chicken — pork this time — along with overcooked green beans and somewhat roasted potatoes. It was the same every time, and the only items that could be ordered individually off of the card were desserts.

"Growing boy," Guy said, patting his stomach.

"Growing boy who looks like hell, by the way."

"You always were such a loving mother."

"Just the truth," Sylvie said. Henri watched it all and couldn't help but smile. The only time his wife ever really became animated anymore, or truly engaged in a conversation anymore, was when one of the kids was around. So he smiled and watched as she speared a potato with her fork and examined it in the light, and then put it back on the plate.

Clarice was absent without explanation. Guy was shoveling in the food faster than seemed human. Henri was focused on the other young person at the table, though, the one sitting at the far end. The one sitting right next to Henri's Uncle Gerard. Name of Nico. Grandson of Gerard, the head of the family.

Sylvie and Henri had been married long enough that she could read his silences pretty often. And so she leaned over and whispered in his ear, "Fucking Nico, eh?"

"Exactly," Henri said.

Nico had appeared out of nowhere a few months before. It really was, poof, I'm your grandson — which was quite a surprise, even to Gerard, seeing as how the old man had never even had a wife. He was well into his seventies and showing his age, but he had never been married. There had always been a story about some girl in his life just before he left for the war in

1917, but there had never been a woman in his life that any of them had seen.

"Never even a whore," is what Sylvie always said.

"You know what I think," is what Guy always said.

"Pop always said there was that one girl," is what Henri always said.

"Then why did he let that priest move in?" is what Guy always said.

"He's just a financial advisor," is what Henri always said about Father Jean Lemieux. For the purposes of these discussions, he always kept the rest of his misgivings about Lemieux to himself.

"The briefcase priest," is what Sylvie always called Lemieux, who kept track of the finances of two pretty different fellows: Gerard La Rue in the house on top of Montmartre and the cardinal in the chancery down by Norte Dame.

"Financial advisor, my ass," is what Guy always said. Then he would mimic someone giving a blowjob, his cheek expanding and then receding, over and over. Then he would say, "Or, maybe, my dear uncle's ass."

"Homos on the brain, that's what you have," is what Henri always said.

"Tell me I'm wrong," is what Guy always said.

"There was always the story of that girl," is what Henri always said.

"Bullshit story, convenient story — like the guys when I was 16 who said their invisible girlfriends went to a different school," is what Guy always said.

That is what they all always said, in a dozen different conversations, until the day a couple of months before when Nico showed up on Gerard's doorstep on the top of the butte. When he showed up with that letter.

2

His mother had been right, of course. Guy really did look like hell. He had been noticing it in the mirror for weeks, noticing it every time he shaved. His skin had become pale. He couldn't remember the last time he'd spent a half-hour on a park bench in the sun. It was apartment to car, car to work, work to after work, after work to bed. It was like that every day. His skin was pale and the dark circles under his eyes were growing bigger and darker. Clarice noticed, too, the last time they'd had a cup of coffee. "Raccoon Randy," is what she had taken to calling her brother.

He looked like shit and he felt like shit. The night before had been a long one, even by recent standards. It was Saturday night, the late night, and the brothels stayed open past midnight — which meant that, by the time Guy and Nico had locked up and begun their own after-work adventures, it was nearer to 1.

They had settled into a pattern on the previous few Saturdays. They needed a late-night place, one with alcohol and women, and Tommy Quinn's was where they were ending up. It was a bar called The Stag. Quinn was an ancient fossil, a Brit who stayed after the first war and who was still on the La Rue family retainer. The bar was more of an old man's kind of place early in the night and an underage kids' place later on — but when it got to be really late, there was a back room where more fun could be had. There also was another back room that was actually a garage, the place where Guy had done his first bit of wet work in the name of the La Rue family. You would think that the memory of his first killing, just a few feet away, would perhaps keep Guy from rising to the occasion with the girls in the back room, but no. Just the opposite, in fact. He tended to get hard as soon as he walked into the bar. And as Guy often thought, exactly how fucked up is that?

Anyway, the back room at The Stag on Saturday night was well staffed, you might say. There were two girls for Guy and three for Nico, and all manner of potential permutations if they had stayed together in the big room — which they had done once but never again, not after Nico grabbed his ass. Accidentally, he said.

Separate or together, though, it was past 4 a.m. when Guy dragged his non-grabbed ass out of there. He had no idea when Nico had left. But eight hours later, the two of them were at the big table in the back room at Vincent's — and damned if Nico didn't look a thousand times better than Guy. Nico was only 22 years old, and all Guy could think was, "Could that four-year gap in their ages possibly make that much of a difference?"

Guy picked up a spoon and looked at his reflection in the back and saw the black circles. Raccoon Randy. Then he looked at Nico and mumbled, "Fresh as a fucking daisy."

When his mother got up and took a walk in the direction of the ladies', Henri scooted over into her seat and whispered into his son's ear. He said, "Just keep his dick wet and blood alcohol high."

"Even if it kills me."

"You're young, and you're loving it."

"I'm exhausted and I have three jobs."

"More like two and a half."

"Tell my body that."

Nico had become Guy's pet project almost from the beginning. It was Henri's idea, and he came to it within a day or two of the shock at Nico's arrival wearing off. Gerard said the kid needed a job, and so he took over a piece of what Guy had been doing at the La Rues' low-rent brothel on Boulevard de Clichy, the whorehouse known universally within the family as "the skank place." So, Guy babysat Gerard's grandson at work, and then he made sure he was entertained after work.

That was Henri's plan. As he said, "Be his boss, be his pimp, be his drinking buddy — whatever it takes. Just keep him happy and keep eyes on him as much as humanly possible."

Guy hadn't had a girlfriend in over a year and there was no way in hell he would ever find the time to acquire one in the current situation. Other than when he was asleep, the rest of Guy's day was at least partially occupied by Nico. And as for the girls every night — maybe six nights a week, with Mondays off for recuperation — Guy was beyond worn out. And then, the last day or so, there was the tingling he felt when taking a piss. He convinced himself it was nothing, but one more day and he would need to find a doctor. Actually, he would just use the one who examined the girls in the La Rue brothels every Wednesday.

Sylvie knew none of this. Well, she knew what Guy did for a living, and where he did it, but Henri hadn't told his wife about the Nico babysitting duties he had added to his son's daily calendar. She just assumed that her son was still her son — that is, hard-working enough but unable to shut off the lights at night, not as long as there was a bar that was still open.

Before she came back from the toilet, Henri leaned in again and whispered, "So, how's he doing at work?"

"Good. Actually, he's doing better than good, since you're asking. That part hasn't been an issue at all. Almost as good as me. Not quite, but almost."

"Goes without saying. And the money?"

"Ticking right along," Guy said. "Not growing but not falling, either. Ticking right along. It's funny. He says it's kind of like when he worked in the shoe store in Lyon. He says, 'Attractive merchandise and attentive customer service — whores and shoes, same fucking difference.'"

Henri nodded. He knew that the envelopes Guy had been delivering hadn't changed since Nico began doing more and more of the running of the skank place. There was always a little variation, but there had been nothing out of the ordinary. It hadn't been that long, but still, nothing out of the ordinary.

Guy picked up the spoon again, looked at himself, and brushed back a bit of hair from his forehead.

"Another thing, and you're not going to like it."

"What?"

"The thing is, I don't hate him," Guy said. "I mean, with everything, he's really a decent guy."

3

The way it worked on Sundays at Vincent's, there was dinner and dessert at the big table, and then the real business of the afternoon took place. For years it had been Gerard and his oldest friend, Silent Moe, who retired to the smaller back room. That was where the envelopes were delivered, in age order: first Henri, then Martin, then Michel. Since forever, each envelope contained two percent off the top — that was Gerard's take as the boss of the family. Only now it was four percent because of that fucking priest. In the past, Moe sat behind Gerard, took the envelopes from Gerard, and said nothing — hence the nickname. Now though, Father Lemieux sat right next to Gerard and participated in every conversation — and took two percent for his trouble. That fucking priest.

Gerard was having a second cup of coffee, so it would be a few minutes. Martin saw that, leaned over the table and said, "Is it done?"

Michel nodded. Motherfucker.

Michel ran the heroin smuggling part of the La Rue family business. He probably brought in three times as much as Martin did from his enterprise — importing liquor and supplying bars and cafés with wine and beer whether they wanted to be supplied or not. Michel was pretty sure he brought in more than Henri, yet they all treated him like shit because he was a cousin from Marseille, not a brother from the goddamned butte, and because he was 10 years younger.

"Was that a yes?" Martin said.

"It was a fucking yes," Michel said.

Martin was an idiot, a stone-cold lunkhead, but Michel had become his pissboy. The latest errand was just that. Martin was involved in a dispute with Roger Black, a man who owned three cafés in the 6th arrondissement. Three cafés, big client — but because he was an incompetent, Martin had tried to push through an unreasonable price increase and had allowed Black's balking to become a little too public. Rather than come to an accommodation, or maybe lean on Black in the customary way — menacing but polite — Martin and his guys just ignored it until Black began organizing a meeting of other café owners in the 5th and 6th. That was when Martin, instead of leaning on Black, leaned on Michel.

"I need him taken care of," Martin said.

"You have people for that."

"They beat up people. They break legs. This, I think, is beyond that."

"I'm not a fucking assassin," Michel said.

"It's just business," Martin said.

And so, it was Martin lying in wait at the back door of one of Roger Black's café. It was Martin perched behind the new model black Citroen. It was Martin who confronted Black when he emerged from the back door, hit him on the head with a hammer, laid him on his stomach, and strangled him with a length of piano wire cut specifically for the task. Michel left the body, and he left the big pouch with the proceeds from the evening's eating and drinking. He thought about stealing it, but that would defeat the purpose. The other café owners needed to know that it hadn't been a robbery that ended the life of poor Roger Black. And even if the cops on the scene took half of the cash from the pouch — even three-quarters, which was likely — they would understand the need to leave at least something behind in the pouch.

Cops liked a good story as well as the next guy, after all, and they knew the newspapers would play up the "it-wasn't-a-robbery" angle. It would sell more newspapers and it would keep the public from getting alarmed. Because, while the man in the street hated random violence, he was entirely in favor of stories about personal vengeance. Jealous lovers were the best but feuding business interests — with a soupçon of mob involvement — worked just fine. And seeing as how the late, lamented Roger Black had been nearing his eighth decade, the whole jealous-lover angle seemed unlikely. Besides, whatever they put in the papers didn't really matter. The other café owners whom Black had been trying to organize — they would know. And that was all that mattered in the end.

Anyway, that was the previous night. Michel had barely slept. The story would be in the Monday papers.

"Any problems?" Martin said.

"What do you fucking care?"

"You hurt me. I care."

"Fuck," Michel said. Fucking lunkhead.

Michel touched his breast pocket, which was where he kept the envelope. Three times bigger than Martin's, easy. Probably four times. The liquor business was shit — at least, the way Martin ran it. It was the idiot's job, unfuck-upable, and yet there always seemed to be a fuck-up of some sort. Both Gerard and Henri thought Martin was useless — you could tell by the way they talked over him at meetings or just ignored what he said.

But it was the La Rue family, and he was a La Rue, and fuck it. Every village has an idiot, and Martin was theirs.

Except for, well, lately. And Michel still couldn't believe he was Martin's pissboy.

There was a noise over to their right. Gerard, Lemieux and Silent Moe were pushing their chairs back from the table. Moe went through the door first, with Gerard next and Lemieux behind him. Always up his fucking ass. Henri gave it 30 seconds and then he followed them in.

"So, it's done, then? Neat and clean?"

"Fucking neat and clean."

"Good to hear," Martin said.

4

Moe sat where Moe always sat — over Gerard's right shoulder, a couple of feet behind. He poured the drinks from the bottle of cognac that had been placed at his own little side table by Vincent himself. You handed Gerard the envelope, he weighed it in his hand, and then he half turned and reached out and Moe took it from him. The handoff accomplished, Gerard would ask questions if he perceived the envelope to be light, or say nothing if he felt it to be appropriate or heavy. There was never a thank you and never an actual counting of how much money was inside.

Of course, the weighing mechanism had become all out of calibration when Gerard decided that his financial/other advisor, the Rev. Jean Fucking Lemieux, was also entitled to two percent of everything — another two percent off the top. So, the envelope was twice its normal size and Gerard would just have to deal with it. Henri drew the line at preparing a separate envelope for the priest and handing it to him, and Gerard never said anything. Maybe he liked it that way. Henri didn't know what Martin and Michel did, and he didn't care — but there was no way he was handing a separate envelope to Lemieux.

But separate envelope or no, the priest was entirely involved in the conversation that followed.

"A little trouble at Gare du Nord," Henri said, as his opening. The truth was, the envelope had been a little light.

"What kind of trouble?" Lemieux said. Gerard leaned forward a few inches but said nothing.

Henri ignored Lemieux and looked directly at his uncle. He said, "Usual shit. Greedy cops."

"But you have an arrangement, no?" It was Lemieux again.

"An arrangement with thieves."

"Police."

"Police who are thieves," Henri said. "Which means the arrangement will always be, how do you say, flexible."

"But..."

"Father, you can't take a crooked cop to court for breach of contract. And you can't kill a crooked cop, Father, except under the most extraordinary circumstances. So what you have to do, Father, is pay the crooked cop what he wants."

Henri made the "Fathers" as disdainful as he could, hoping Gerard would get from the repeated punctuation what a naive fool his new advisor was. But Gerard's face betrayed nothing. And as for Lemieux, he seemed to be entirely uninsultable. His face never changed, and he pressed on with a half-dozen more stupid questions that didn't stop until Henri stopped him.

"It's fucking done, Father, and it will be coming out of the envelope for the foreseeable future," he said.

"Until when?"

"Until I can get the greedy police captain transferred to somebody else's precinct, to someone else's train station."

"When?"

"Four months, maybe six."

"Seems long."

"I don't run the cops' personnel department, for Christ's sake," Henri said.

The silence that followed was prolonged; it was Gerard who finally ended it. He asked a question about Nico, about how his grandson was doing, and Gerard's face betrayed part concern and part, well, joy. It was the oddest look — concern with the eyes, joy with the mouth.

"Fine, from what I can tell," Henri said. No more praiseworthy than that.

Gerard seemed to relax at that point. He was looking well overall, not gray and sickly like he had before they had all gone to Lourdes at Lemieux's insistence. Fucking Lourdes. For months Gerard had seemed as if was on a slow boat to the grave, refusing to see a doctor despite his decline. His recovery could be tracked exactly with the trip to Lourdes, as could Lemieux's rise from Gerard's semi-official personal financial advisor to his quite-official right-hand man — with two percent off the top to prove it. Fucking Lourdes.

And Lemieux wasn't done.

"But what about Guy?" the priest said.

"What about him?"

"He has new responsibilities."

"And, so?"

"Are you sure he's up to them?"

"Now you listen," Henri said. "Guy is my employee."

"Guy is your son who's also an employee."

"And he's more than capable of handling the responsibilities that he has been given," Henri said.

Neither Gerard nor Lemieux knew about the final added responsibility, the one where Guy was required to be Nico's running buddy until the small hours every night/morning. That last job was a secret between father and son.

"It seems a lot for a young man."

"He's a very capable young man," Henri said. And then he stared down Lemieux, stared him into silence, stared until the priest's eyes dropped.

Gerard said nothing.

5

W hether it was Chrétien contacting Henri or Henri contacting Chrétien, the procedure was the same. It consisted of a telephone message saying that Mr. Brown was seeking a meeting at such-and-such a time. Always Mr. Brown, either way.

Given that it was a Sunday, Chrétien wouldn't be working — but that wasn't a problem. When Henri called and left the message — "Mr. Brown, 4 p.m." — it was taken at the precinct and then delivered by a kid on a motorbike to wherever Chrétien was. He had to leave his whereabouts with the desk sergeant at all times, as did every police captain, and there was a kid on a motorbike assigned to every police precinct in the city.

They always met at the little park on Rue Burq, the one that kind of dead-ended into nowhere about halfway up the butte. Given that it was a Sunday, the park was busier than on weekdays. Also, given that it was a Sunday, that meant it was Daddy Duty Day. And so, while the kids ran around and jumped and climbed on the playground equipment in the back of the park, a half-dozen fathers lounged on the benches and passed a bottle around. And so, an uproarious shout of man-laughter occasionally pierced the low-level but constant high-pitched chatter of the children.

Henri arrived first and chose a bench near the entrance to the park, away from the playground. It was beside a vast, flat dirt rectangle that would have been perfect for boules — but Henri had never seen anyone playing. He heard one of the bursts of man-laughter and looked back over his shoulder. None of the men passing around the bottle looked back.

When Chrétien arrived, five minutes later, he was dressed in his Sunday clothes — checked slacks, open shirt, brown jacket.

"Mimi will kill me if I miss dinner," he said. He looked at his watch and shook his head.

"What's on the menu?"

"Leg of lamb."

"With roasted potatoes?"

"And mint jelly."

"Lucky," Henri said. The truth was that Sylvie as a cook was equal parts mediocre and disinterested. He couldn't remember the last time she had prepared a leg of lamb.

"Five minutes," Henri said. "Ten minutes, tops."

At which point, Henri laid out his request — which was more of an order than a request. After all, Chrétien was the working definition of a bought-and-paid-for police captain. The envelopes that Henri handed him on a quarterly basis were enough to pay for a new car every year as well as an annual Chrétien family vacation to Brittany.

Still, Henri knew, the guy had his pride — even if he was bought-and-paid-for. So there was always a little dance, and Henri was willing to tolerate it.

"I need for you to get in touch with one of your cop friends in Lyon, and to get him to do some investigative work for me."

Chrétien began his dance with, "Lyon? What, you think all cops know each other? Like we were all birthed from the same womb, fed from the same tit?"

"I pay you enough for the womb, both tits and whatever else I deem necessary," Henri said. Two to tango, after all.

He handed Chrétien a piece of paper containing all the basic information that he knew about Nico. Chrétien then went with his next bit, the physical theatrics. First, there was the objection. Second, there was the visible straining, as if Henri was asking him to birth a calf. It was always like that, verbal objection followed by physical angst.

This time, it manifested itself with a theatrical closing of the eyes and turning his face toward the sky, followed by a close reading of the piece of paper that involved a painful amount of squinting.

And then Chrétien said, "Well, I might know a guy."

As Henri knew he would.

"But here's the thing. Cops don't really do this kind of thing. You want name, address, driver's license, arrest record — a cop can get you that without a lot of trouble. But I get the sense you're looking for more, yes?"

Henri nodded.

"Cops really don't do that, and this kind of thing really isn't covered by, well, by our agreement."

"Our agreement covers whatever I say it fucking covers," Henri said. The dance was over.

Chrétien dropped the theatrics but repeated his point. He said, "I'm telling you, cops really don't do this kind of thing. Private investigators do this kind of thing."

Henri thought for a second.

"Well, get your cop friend in Lyon off your mother's tit for five minutes and have him recommend a private investigator for me."

"When?"

"Today. Immediately. And when you're done, the lamb will taste even better."

PART II

6

——————

Clarice had missed Sunday at Vincent's in order to spend Sunday in Pierre's bed. Pierre, the professional student who was endlessly pursuing a doctorate in history that would earn him fuck-all in the end. Pierre, the Jewish boyfriend who was living off his parents, living in a flat in the same building where Hemingway and one of his wives first lived.

Between the bouts of sex — there would be three of them in about eight hours that day — Pierre would wrap himself in a towel and pad down the hall in his bare feet to, as he liked to say, "Piss in Ernie's pot." When he came back — it was after the second time — Clarice asked him, "How much do you get from them in a month?"

"How much what? And who's 'them?'"

"How much is money, and them is your parents."

"You mean the people you never want to meet?"

"What's the point?"

"Why does there need to be a point? Dinner, a few drinks, daddy picks up the check — there doesn't need to be a point beyond that."

"We've talked about this — why bother?" Clarice said.

Their relationship was perfect in so many ways. They were very relaxed together, comfortable with silence. The sex was spectacular and creative — and the creativity was all on Pierre's part. The last thing he did, with his tongue and then his finger and then his tongue again, left her gasping and wondering where he learned this stuff. From a book? Or was there a teacher? Part of her was desperate to find out, especially if there was a teacher. Part of her, though, didn't care.

They laughed together, and she always looked forward to their meetings. She didn't call it love, though, didn't permit the thought to enter her head, because of, well, the obvious. Pierre was Jewish, and that meant it wasn't going to work for either of their families. He knew it, she knew it, and they didn't really even talk about it very much. It was what it was — so, they settled for fucking three times in eight hours. She hardly considered that settling.

"But really, how much do you get from them each month?" Clarice said.

Pierre told her.

"Will they give you three months in advance? Like, if you tell them you can get a break on the rent that way, or some such shit?"

Pierre said that, yes, he likely could get them to do it. At which point, a kind of dirty smile formed on his lips. Clarice was a broker, and he knew what kind of broker — the kind that wasn't all that concerned about the rules surrounding what was and wasn't an acceptable trade of securities. Pierre also knew that she was a La Rue, and what that all entailed. They never really talked about it, about sleeping with the daughter of a crime boss, but Pierre had an imagination. And the way Clarice figured it, his imagination wouldn't cover the half of it when it came to the business side of the La Rue family.

"Call them tonight, get the three months' worth," she said. "You won't regret it. But you'll need it by, say, Thursday."

"And you're not going to tell me any more than that?"

"You know all you need to know," she said. And then she pushed his head down in the general direction of where his tongue and his finger had been the last time.

7

They were back in the house that sat in the private street that ran behind Sacré Coeur, the house that would have comfortably slept eight but which was occupied by only two, by Gerard and his personal priest/advisor. Before he had gone home to have dinner with his wife, Silent Moe had done the division from the envelopes and prepared an envelope for Lemieux. He left it on the little side table next to the fussy Louis XIV chair upon which Gerard always sat in the drawing room, the chair that faced the Van Gogh.

"A minor work, but still," is what Gerard always said, whenever he saw somebody noticing the painting and sometimes even when they weren't.

One time — one time too many in Henri's thinking — he responded by asking Gerard, "Have you ever had its authenticity tested."

"What the fuck are you saying?"

"Nothing, nothing. But it can be a shady business, the art trade. Have you ever been supplied with the painting's provenance?"

"Get the fuck out of here, provenance."

"I was just wondering," Henri said. He was wondering because he knew that, while Gerard had received the painting from a reputable gallery, well, let's just say that it did not exit the place out the front door in broad daylight.

Anyway, Gerard never brought up the painting in Henri's presence anymore. Father Lemieux, though, was different. The last time the priest had asked about it, Gerard gave him 10 minutes on the evolution of Van Gogh's brush strokes through the decades. And when Henri walked in on the two of them, before a family meeting, he overheard the last of it and thought to himself, "Yeah, stroke this, old man."

But there was no talk of the painting that night. Each sipped from a glass of cognac, Lemieux with the bulging envelope sitting in his lap. Gerard was in a generous mood, full of praise for the priest.

"Jean, your wisdom — I don't know what I would do without it."

"You would do what you've always done — guide your nephews, your entire family, to such great success."

"Don't kid a kidder."

"I'm not."

"You are," Gerard said. "I'm slower. I know it."

"Physically slower, maybe, although I wouldn't want to arm wrestle with you."

"Not just physically, and you know it. The only reason the rest of them don't know it is because of you. It's you who carries my conversations now. It's you who lays out the alternatives in a few seconds — something that would take me much longer."

"But you still make the decisions," Lemieux said. "I merely arrange the paperwork, get it in order."

"Perhaps," Gerard said. He sipped, and the two of them fell into a companionable silence.

Perhaps, my ass — that's what Lemieux thought. He sipped,

and he felt the envelope, and that's what went through his head. Perhaps, my ass.

The whole thing, months in the making, could not have gone any better. The arsenic in the jars of preserves that Gerard slathered on his bread every morning — not enough to kill, just enough to slowly poison the old man's system — had worked exactly as Lemieux had been told. Gerard's skin turned pale and then gray, and his digestion went to shit, so to speak. He grew tired and irritable, and he did nothing about it because he hated doctors. His decline was obvious to everyone, including himself, but Gerard would take no action to try to find out what was wrong. The only thing Lemieux could get him to do was the one thing he was sure the old man who walked the block to Sacré Coeur for Mass every morning would agree on. That is, the trip to Lourdes. And that it coincided with the replacement of the arsenic-tainted preserves with some unadulterated jars, well...

It went just as he had hoped. As he recovered, Gerard gave the credit to Lourdes and to Lemieux for making the suggestion. And given that he had been there throughout Gerard's decline — first as someone who helped keep his personal ledgers in order, then with more and more — a kind of dependence had been created. He never even had to suggest the separate envelope, his own two percent.

He felt the envelope again and said, "Gerard, about Nico."

"What about him?"

"He makes you happy, yes?"

"Very."

"I can tell — it's a blessing, happiness."

"One of many blessings in my life, including you."

Gerard poured each of them another small measure of the cognac. Until Nico started receiving an envelope of his own, Father Lemieux decided that even though the kid was a complication, he wasn't going to worry about the grandson who dropped in from heaven.

8

Freddy arranged the snapshots on the desk, turned upside down but facing the visitor's chair. He was in the office above the luggage store. The window behind him overlooked the Place de la République. The statue of Marianne was right there. It sometimes felt like it was almost close enough to touch.

Captain Rodrique Merced was five minutes late, as was his custom. His way of showing his superiority. Except, well, Henri had decided that enough was enough with the whole superiority business, along with the demands for a raise.

The white envelope, sealed as always, sat on the desk next to the upside-down photographs. The customary glasses of cognac were already poured. This monthly dance was always choreographed, always just so. This time, the photographs were the only difference.

There were six pictures in all. Two of them were of Merced's wife, Gillian. In one, she was wrestling a bag of groceries while simultaneously trying to unlock the door of their apartment in the 17th. It was over by Square des Batignolles where Henri said he sometimes played boules. In the second, a man was helping

Gillian with the groceries and then taking a step inside the apartment house to follow her. The next two pictures were of Merced's two children, a boy and girl, about 8 and 10. They were outside the apartment wearing their school uniforms. They probably came from the La Rue shop on Avenue de Clichy. The final two pictures were of the family pet, a little weasel of a dog that the kids were chasing on the street.

Merced sat down, as usual. He took a drink of the cognac, as usual. He sliced open the envelope with a pocketknife, as usual.

"I thought we discussed this," Merced said. The amount of money had not changed from the previous month, despite the demand.

Freddy said nothing in reply. Instead, he turned over the pictures, one by one — wife and groceries, wife and groceries and new assistant, children in school uniforms, children chasing dog.

"What the fuck is this?" Merced said.

"It's exactly what you think it is."

"You fucking—"

"He's one of my guys," Freddy said. He tapped the photograph with the man carrying the groceries into the apartment. "And in case you were wondering, his dick is this big."

Freddy held his hands a foot apart.

Merced looked at all six photographs again.

"If you fucking think this gives you some kind of leverage—"

"I don't think, I know," Freddy said.

The way Henri had explained it, cops were indeed untouchable, even crooked cops who were getting more than a little bit greedy. You couldn't hurt them and you couldn't really threaten to turn them in to their bosses — because pretty much everybody who wore a blue uniform was likely getting a taste from somebody. The bosses couldn't abide pressure being applied from the La Rue end — it would upset their delicate ecosystem.

The cops' response would be to shut down the La Rues until they buckled — and they would buckle eventually, and everybody on both sides knew it.

"So, that won't work," Henri said. "But if we go for the wife instead..."

"Kill her?" Freddy said.

"No, fuck her."

"Like, literally?"

"Yes, literally," Henri said. "Put one of those young lunkheads you have working for you on it. She's pushing 40, so send a 25-year-old on the mission. It shouldn't take very long."

"But doesn't he still have the leverage? I mean, one word to his boss and he could still shut us down."

"He would have the leverage, except he won't," Henri said.

"I don't get it."

"He only has the leverage if he's willing to tell his boss that your lunkhead is fucking his wife. And, well, I don't know the man — but if he's like every other man in this magnificent city, and probably any city, there is no way in hell that he's going to tell his boss that the reason he has a problem with the La Rue family is that one of the La Rue lunkheads is feeding his dick to his wife while Merced is at work."

Which was, as it turned out, exactly the truth. Merced accepted what was in the envelope — which was actually a five percent decrease from the previous month — without further comment. The cop scooped up the six photographs and stuffed them into the same pocket with the envelope, and that was fine with Freddy. The five percent discount had been his idea, something Henri didn't need to know. As for Henri, well, Gerard and that goddamned priest would continue to take a lighter envelope for the next six months, until Henri could arrange for Merced's transfer to a different precinct.

9

The uniform store on Avenue de Clichy was one of the three legitimate arms of the La Rue family business. There was the luggage store in the 10th that they inherited along with the Gare du Nord when the Morel family imploded, and there was the wine and spirits importing business that Martin ran, and there was the uniform store.

"The biggest supplier of school uniforms in Paris," is what it said on the sign in the front window, and that was true enough. But it was a tiny piece of the overall income of the family, a slender sliver — and the wine importing operation and the luggage store were even smaller. Crumbs. But the three businesses served their purpose — that is, to supply legitimate tax numbers and health insurance credentials to all of the La Rue family employees.

The other two kind of ran themselves, but the uniform supply company had real employees — seamstresses and delivery people and order-takers — and was a complete pain in the ass. It was Passy's complete pain in the ass. The way Henri always figured it, given that Passy had the highest income operation on a weekly basis — the casino at Trinity One — the pain in the ass was a fair trade-off. He would work a couple of hours in the afternoon at the uniform store, a couple of hours after that at Trinity One, and collect a lot more than Timmy and Freddy for his trouble.

Since the heart attack, though, Passy was limiting himself to a few hours at the uniform store. That was where Guy came in.

The conversation had been easier than Henri had expected — which told him, or at least suggested, that Passy's health was worse than he was letting on. There had been this confluence of complications — what to do with Nico, and what to do with Passy — and Henri decided that Guy could solve them both provided that Passy didn't throw a fit.

And, he didn't. He almost seemed relieved when Henri laid it out for him.

"Look, you need to rest and recover," he said. They were sitting in his office in the back of the uniform store. The door was closed, and the constant thrum of the sewing machines and shouts of the delivery guys were muted.

"Here's what I'm thinking. You work a few hours a day in here, just to keep the place running and keep all of us good with the tax man. Then you go home for dinner and put your feet up and watch television. Guy will take your place at Trinity One. You'll advise him and be available for him on the phone if there's an issue."

"And?" Passy said. It was the only time there was even a hint of concern on his face. It disappeared immediately, though, when Henri told him that he would keep 75 percent of what he had been earning and that Guy would get the other 25 percent. Not only did the concern disappear — it was replaced by a smile.

They shook hands, and Henri was relieved in one sense. At least in the short term, the problem had been solved. Guy would give up a piece of his income from the two brothels to pay Nico, and he would do the same oversight at the skank place that Passy would be doing for him at Trinity One. But the 25 percent of the Trinity One casino money was more than triple what he would be paying Nico, so Guy would be more than happy to do the extra work, at least for a while.

So, all settled. Still, Henri was worried. Passy was suddenly looking very much like a shot fighter. He had seen it with other guys, his father's guys. One by one they had become facsimiles of themselves. They got into their fifties and they just didn't have the stomach for some of it, the stomach or the stamina.

Passy was 53 and looked it, even before the heart attack. Timmy was 51 and honestly looked 10 years younger. He would joke about "the elixir of life," and then make a V with his fingers and begin licking through the opening, and everybody would laugh.

The problem was that Timmy's judgment was, well, pretty much non-existent — his idea of prudence was a monthly shot of penicillin in one ass cheek and a weekly dose of B-12 in the other. Passy was the wise head, the one Henri relied on. If Passy retired or died, Henri really wouldn't have anyone — except maybe Sylvie. Christ.

10

Martin always came for his extra collection to the garage where Michel had initially stored the heroin, the secret heroin. It was long gone, the secret heroin, but that didn't really matter. The garage, which also served as a place for Michel to store vehicles used in the business, was the place and would likely always be the place.

Martin insisted that it be a version of the back room at Vincent's — minus Silent Moe and the priest. He instructed Michel to have a table, two chairs, a bottle of cognac, and two glasses. Oh, and the envelope, which Martin always weighed in his hand the way Gerard did. The only difference was that he opened it and counted it in front of Michel. He knew the correct amount because it was half of what Martin had already received as his quarterly share of the family profits.

That Michel seethed during the whole thing was worth almost as much as the cash. Almost. So Martin always dragged it out for at least 10 minutes. He fumbled with the envelope. He counted slowly. He drank slowly. And if Michel normally rifled three measures of cognac in the time it took him to drain one, all the better. That day, he drank four — fine. If he needed the extra anesthetic — again, fine. Michel's balls were in Martin's pocket and they were going to stay there. The goddamned self-important weasel.

What Martin couldn't know, mostly because he wasn't much of a deep thinker or much of a student of the human condition, was that he was in danger of pushing his younger cousin beyond the imaginary line between tolerance and intolerance, between anger and action. A smarter man would have seen that you can only push a man so far, even if his balls are in your pocket. All Martin could feel, though, were a full pocket and full envelope.

He had caught Michel cheating on the family, and as he told his cousin, "You fuck the La Rues, the La Rues fuck you."

"I am a La Rue," Michel said.

"So, we fuck you harder," Martin said.

They were in Lourdes, and Michel was in the middle of a heroin deal gone bad — a deal involving stolen heroin about which Michel had not informed the family, a side deal that Gerard and Henri would have killed him for. Or, maybe, beat the shit out of him and sent him back to Marseille. Or, if he was the luckiest cheating scumbag in France, maybe turned him into Henri's assistant and taken away 90 percent of his income for the same work.

But Martin saved Michel that night and killed four men in the process. Martin saved him and then he fucked him hard. In exchange for his silence, Martin received half of Michel's quarterly profit sharing and also took great pleasure in turning Michel into his errand boy. That Roger Black business in the alley behind his café had just been the latest. And there was nothing Michel could do about it.

As he drank the fourth cognac, and watched as Martin counted the money a second time, Michel wondered, though. Why not just fucking kill him?

He knew the reason — Martin, the idiot, said he had sent a

letter from the hotel in Lourdes, right when they were checking out on the morning after the night before. The letter detailed everything, and he promised it would find its way to Gerard and Henri if anything happened to him. It was his insurance, the ingenious asshole.

But it had been months. And for all he knew, the letter had been a bluff. And even if it hadn't been a bluff, well, what would happen if Martin had a heart attack a year after Lourdes? Or got hit by a taxi on the Champs? Would the letter still somehow get to Gerard and Henri? Christ.

Michel was pouring a fifth cognac when Martin got up and announced he was headed to the bathroom. About two minutes later, the bathroom door opened and Martin stood there with his pants around his ankles.

"Paper," he yelled. Then he went back inside.

Michel sat there and drank the cognac in one. Fuck him.

"Paper," Martin yelled, this time from behind the closed door.

Martin wanted to tell him to use the cash from the envelope, but didn't.

"Don't have any," he yelled back.

"Market's right next door," Martin yelled in return.

Michel sat there, staring at the bottle. He sat there and thought about all of it — the heroin side deal that was long finished, the hundreds of thousands of francs that Martin had extorted from him, the letter that did or did not exist, the truth — the very real truth — that the La Rues would probably lose half of their income if they put a bullet in his brain as revenge for what was, in reality, just a little bit of industriousness on his part.

He weighed it, all of it.

He took a swig from the bottle.

And then Michel stood up and walked next door to the market to buy his idiot cousin a roll of toilet paper. And while he was paying for it, he promised that he would a way out of his indignity.

11

H e had lived in the apartment for more than a decade, two floors in a building with an elevator on a private street in the shadow of Sacré Coeur. It was literally in the shadow for at least part of most mornings. If he looked out of the window from the top floor, from the very top of the butte, he could see a slice of the view that tourists enjoyed from the steps in front of the basilica. He could remember when they started the construction, when he was a little kid. He could remember when the whole thing was still covered by scaffolding, back when he got on the train in his uniform, the train that led to a dozen more trains, the train that led to Verdun. God, he was old.

The apartment had four bedrooms, big enough to sleep eight comfortably, 10 if you put people on couches, not that he ever had. The only other person who slept there regularly was Jean Lemieux — a couple of nights a week when he started helping Gerard get his ledgers together after several years of neglect, now six nights a week. Their friendship had started when Lemieux had been an assistant pastor at St. Peter's, the church that was so close to Sacré Coeur, just across a narrow street, that the joke was the pastor at St. Peter's and the rector at Sacré Coeur could sit on their respective toilets and trade magazines out the window when they were finished with the last page. When Lemieux got transferred out of St. Peter's, it was to go downtown where he watched over the cardinal's books as he did over Gerard's.

It was Thursday night, the one night of the week when Lemieux slept in his room at the rectory near Notre Dame. Maurice had gone home to have dinner with his wife, and Gerard was left alone with the creaks and groans of the old building, along with the occasional police siren during the summer, when the tourists sometimes required a bit of herding. It was just him and the noises and the Van Gogh — and for most of the decade, it had been enough. But since Lemieux had moved in, it was different — the quiet quieter, the creaks and the groans a little more jarring. He tended to check to make sure the front door was locked now after dinner, something he had never done before. The back door behind the kitchen, too, although Clara never forgot to lock it after she got done cleaning up and packaging the leftovers.

He listened to the news on the radio in the far corner of the drawing room, far away from the Van Gogh. He was late and missed the main headlines. They were doing a story about the American election, and he listened for a minute. The Democrats had just picked Kennedy, and there was talk of a wave of excitement at their convention in Los Angeles.

And Gerard muttered to no one, "His main qualification is that people want to fuck his wife. It's not enough."

He actually heard the last word echo in the empty room and realized he was talking to himself. Whatever. He snapped off the radio and walked back across the room to the Louis XIV chair where he usually sat. And then Gerard did what he had taken to doing on Thursday nights when the house was empty. He reached into the drawer of the little side table and pulled out the envelope.

It had been white when it was manufactured but the decades had turned it yellow. The note was written on that really thin paper they used for airmail letters to reduce the weight. If you held it up to the light, you could almost see through it. But it had stayed white, even since 1919.

Nico had brought it as his only means of identification. He had no driver's license, no papers of any kind when he arrived from Lyon. Just the letter in the yellowed envelope. Nico had held it in his right hand as he stood there at the door, at the apartment on the private street in the shadow of Sacré Coeur.

Gerard unfolded it carefully, and put on his glasses, and began to read. The house was empty, and this was now what he did.

My dearest Gerard,

You are two months old as I write this, two months exactly, 61 days old. I will die on the 62nd day, most likely. No later than the 63rd.

I have contracted what the newspapers have taken to calling the Spanish flu. It is a terrible disease, a true scourge. I had felt sick just two days ago. I threw up some blood and the nuns knew almost immediately. There had been another girl, maybe six months ago. The nuns put me in the same room. They slipped this paper and a pencil beneath the door.

I feel it is important that you know the truth about your heritage. I hope someday you will be able to understand. I am your mother, Celeste Lemaire. Your name is Gerard Lemaire. You are named after your father, Gerard La Rue. I hope he got back from the war, and that you will meet him one day. He is from Paris.

That is where I am from, too. My parents sent me here when the doctor said I was with child. I was not married, and my parents feared the scandal. If you do not understand, there will be someone to explain.

They sent me to live in a convent in Lyon that had been suggested by our pastor in Paris. The nuns were truly holy women who were dedicated to assisting girls in my situation. I gave birth in their convent, and they said you screamed louder than any child they could remember. A good omen, I believed.

You slept well and ate well from the start. We had yet to determine my next move when the Spanish flu arrived. Now, there will be no need. I guess I will be buried here, in the convent's yard. I had read a newspaper story recently about the need to burn the bodies of Spanish flu victims, but I don't know. There is no one to ask at this point, and I hope not.

As I said, I hope you will get to meet your father one day. Gerard La Rue is a smart man, a kind man. If I remember correctly, his unit was the Third Army, 6th Corps. I hope he survived, and that you will meet him some day. I am sure he will love you, despite the years and the distance. I am sure because that is the kind of man he is, and the kind of man I hope you will be.

You are named after him.

Love, Celeste

Your mother

Every time he read the letter, Gerard cried. Then he folded it up, put it back in the yellowed envelope, put the envelope in the drawer, took off his glasses, and turned off the light in the drawing room. The last thing he saw was the Van Gogh. The last thing he heard was the creaking as he walked up the steps to his bedroom, the fourth step in particular.

PART III

12

"You check in alone?" Martin said.

"This is stupid," Marie said. She caught her breath and wiped her face, and then she devolved to her standard attitude, the one where her husband was an idiot. She tried to be supportive, but there were times...

"Just fucking do it, all right?" he said.

"It's eight in the morning. They're not going to have a room."

He handed her a wad from his pocket.

"They'll have a fucking room. A suite."

"Maiden name?"

"Right. I'll call up in 10 minutes and you tell me the room number. Get two keys."

"And a single woman will need two keys for exactly what reason?"

"Right, right, one key," Martin said.

He sat at the lobby bar in the George V and ordered a whisky. There were two other guys there, too. It always amazed him how early people drank when they were staying in a hotel. At least he had a reason.

How had this happened? He knew he had to call Gerard and

tell him, because there were protocols for this kind of thing in the La Rue family, but screw it. It could wait a few more minutes. After eight hours, what were a few more minutes? Besides, it wasn't like it was his fault. He would drink his drink, and get up to the room, and call from there.

The whole thing had been so simple in the planning. These guys, the five of them, they were amateurs, after all. Kids. Punks. Numb-nuts. That's what Martin used to call Guy's crew when they first started out. Numb-nuts. Or was it knuckleheads? Whatever — that was these five guys. When he saw them the first time, he was pretty sure they were wearing the first nice suits they had ever owned — and on two of them, the pants were floods. Numb-nuts.

They acted like free agents. They never said anything about the Garreaus, who nominally ran the 6th. It was kind of a free territory, the 6th, at least when it came to the bars and the cafés. It was a first-come, first-served kind of arrangement. Martin had his bars, the Garreaus had their bars, and so did a couple other families. It was one of those old-time agreements among the families whose origin was a mystery. The Garreaus had the brothel and most of the alcohol in the arrondissement, but the rest were grandfathered in — and while the bar owners sometimes switched their allegiances among the families, and it was legal in their world, the switching was discouraged. Lead pipes, brass knuckles, the odd bullet in the knee — discouraged.

And so, when word got back to one of Martin's guys that there were these five punks asking at a few of the La Rue places if they were satisfied with their arrangements, Martin began to rage.

"Who the fuck are they?" he said.

"Just kids," his guy said.

"Names?"

His guy shrugged.

"They need to be stopped now."

His guy nodded.

"I mean, stopped," Martin said. "Fucking stopped. Permanently fucking stopped. They don't get to grow up to be adults — that kind of stopped. Nobody does this to the La Rues. Do you fucking understand?"

His guy nodded.

They were easy enough to spot, the numb-nuts. They didn't try to hide what they were doing. It was like they were working off of a list of La Rue cafés, and they just went from one to the next along Rue Saint-Sulpice. Three of Martin's men watched from a distance. It was after they left the second café, The Parrot, when they blasted the five numb-nuts with shotguns from across the street.

It was only the next morning, when the captain on Martin's payroll called the apartment on Avenue Montaigne, that they found out that Martin's men had winged one of the numb-nuts and killed another. That was fine, in and of itself. It would have been plenty to discourage these free-agent punks or anybody else like them.

It would have, except for the fact that the numb-nuts in question were not free agents. The dead one was Jean Garreau, grandson of Sylvain Garreau, head of the Garreau family, who were nominally in charge of the 6th.

"And you're telling me this because?" Martin said. Denial was all he could think.

"Don't kid a kidder," his cop said.

"I don't know what you're talking about."

"Look, I've known you a long time, and you've known me. And if I can add two and two, so can the Garreaus."

"Your two-and-two is equaling five," Martin said.

His cop sighed.

"Don't say I didn't warn you," he said.

As soon as he hung up, Martin began screaming at Marie to begin packing. He called his driver and told him to park the car on Rue Bayard — Martin and Marie would get to it through the back alley. Marie was flinging underwear and two dresses into a single bag, and Martin tossed a suit and some underwear on top of the pile. The lid barely closed. As he got dressed, Martin peeked out the front window, the one that looked out onto Avenue Montaigne. It was a fabulous apartment, out of the decorator magazines, and it was conveniently close to the Champs but far enough away that you couldn't hear the traffic noise. In the middle of the block. Chanel was across the street.

There was a car parked right in front of the apartment with two guys sitting in it. One of them was wearing a sling on his arm. As Martin knotted his tie, a second car pulled up and parked right behind the first one. That one also had two guys in it.

"Come on, come on," Martin yelled, and Marie took the stairs quickly while carrying her shoes. Martin was right behind her, lugging the suitcase. He was just slamming the back door behind him when he heard the first of four blasts that had to have come from shotguns, from the four men parked across the street. Two drivers, two passengers, four shooters. He heard the blasts and the broken glass, and then Martin didn't hear anything other than his wife's screams.

13

Guy woke up refreshed. He had begged off an after-hours drink with Nico for the first time, and the early night seemed to supply him with a shot of adrenaline. There was none of the customary fog when he opened his eyes, no desire to turn over for another half-hour after he checked the little windup clock on the nightstand.

"Sleep, the best tonic," he thought. Unless, of course, if the tonic had been the other thing.

He showered and dressed and thought about the night before at Trinity One. It had begun days earlier — no, weeks — when Passy had called him and told him about this one punter who kept grabbing the waitresses. This was an unusual problem in the casino. Upstairs in the brothel, you got the occasional lunkhead who thought he owned one of the girls, not just rented, and you dealt with it by throwing his ass out on the street — preferably naked, with the clothing eventually tossed out of the window and onto the sidewalk. Taking aim with the shoes in that circumstance was entirely appropriate.

Down in the casino, the problems were almost always guys in so deep as to be drowning financially. There was a playbook there — warnings, followed by physical warnings, followed by really physical warnings, followed by banishment accompanied by whatever it took to recover the debt.

But this guy, this Jean Luc, was different. Passy said he had warned him a half-dozen times, but eventually the warnings would wear off and Jean Luc would grab another waitress. The girls were really sick of it and had called Passy to complain, which led to the most recent warning. As Passy said, "I mean, a pinch here or there is still thought of as coloring inside the lines — and the girls honestly do get that. But this Jean Luc, he's cornering them, backing them up against the wall. It has to stop, and he's been told. Next time."

Well, this was the next time. The brunette waitress, Corinne, yelped loud enough that the whole place turned and saw the end of her encounter with Jean Luc. He was doubled over, likely having just endured a knee to the ball sack. She was straightening her skirt and emerging from the corner next to the bar. Guy looked at Corinne, and she stared at him with an undisguised fury on her face. Guy mouthed the words, "I got it," and patted himself on the chest with his open right hand.

The two bouncers and one of the two bartenders corralled Jean Luc and hustled him down the back stairs, the ones that led to the alley behind the building. There was only a single bulb fixture that lit the space, and it was more in shadow than light, but Guy would see the fear on Jean Luc's face when he came through the back door. He heard the cinders crunch beneath his feet as he walked over to where the boys were holding Jean Luc, the cinders and then the breathing that bordered on whimpering.

"What's the worry, big man?" Guy said.

Jean Luc didn't answer.

"Big man with the women," Guy said. Then he whispered something to the bartender, who approached their wriggling captive and undid his belt and pants, lowering them along with the underpants.

"Full marks for not pissing yourself, at least not yet," Guy said. "But for such a big man with the waitresses, you have an awfully shriveled dick here in the alley."

Jean Luc actually looked down, then closed his eyes. Guy looked at the two bouncers and said, "Hold him up, boys."

They got him to his feet, and each of them held Jean Luc beneath an armpit, and then Guy removed his coat and rolled up his sleeves and began whaling away — fists to the face, a kick in the balls, and then when the bouncers dropped him and Jean Luc landed on his knees, Guy pushed him back against the brick wall with a shove delivered by the bottom of his shoe on Jean Luc's pathetic face.

"Oops, pissed himself," Guy said.

Jean Luc was in a daze, lying there. He tried to sit up but only succeeded in making himself sick.

"Puke on your dick, I bet that burns," Guy said.

With that, he backed away from his handiwork and began to get dressed again, rolling down his sleeves and then putting on his jacket.

"Needless to say, he's banned," Guy said. He was talking to one of the bouncers. The other bouncer and the bartender were starting to drag Jean Luc out to the street, his heels digging parallel shallow trenches in the cinders.

"Boss," the bouncer said.

"Yeah."

"That's our job, boss."

Guy shrugged.

"Seriously, Guy," the bouncer said. His name was Ronald, and they were the same age. "You're the boss and you need to act like it. We like working for you — more than Passy. But you can't blur the lines — well, maybe a little, but not too much."

"So, that time we shared that what's-her-name upstairs…"

"Maybe a little," Ronald said. "But, like I said, not too much. I mean, you went first."

"Well, I am the fucking boss."

They both laughed. Guy understood what he was saying, though. And while the two of them watched Jean Luc's heels digging the railroad tracks in the cinders, Guy said, "Thanks for the advice. But I need to keep my hand in. Besides, there's plenty to go around."

All of that ran through Guy's head as he showered and dressed the next morning. God, he felt great. And while he didn't dwell on it, he was self-aware enough to wonder, just for a minute, how much of the freshness he was feeling had been the sleep and how much had been the alley.

14

They were at The Parquet, one of the three bars on the side street closest to the bourse. Part of the floor was from the original bourse, or so they said. It was where the brokers went most days after the markets closed — most for one drink, some for two on a particularly negative day for shares, some for a half-dozen because of the conviviality among the group of brokers and the prospect of what was waiting for them at home.

Clarice had three drinks that day and paid for none of them. There had been no way to hide her share purchases anymore, and the other brokers came alone or in small groups to ask a variation of the same question.

Or, as Paul Montreaux said — Montreaux wore threadbare suits and barely seemed to survive as a broker — "What the fuck is up with Riom?"

The Riom Mining Company was located in the Massif Central, close to the Alps but not quite there, along a lazy river that was a tributary to the Rhône. It wasn't a mom-and-pop organization — the shares had been listed on the bourse since 1911, after all — but it was as mom-and-pop-ish as a public company could possibly be. The filings said the company had 1,225 employees and a five-man board of directors, three with the last name of Arnaud. Its earnings grew a little bit most years — less than five percent, never more — and fell a bit during recessions. Mostly it extracted lead and silver from mineral veins that the company said would be sufficient for the next fifty years. Which was a guess on their part, she guessed.

The stock was the definition of sleepy. It paid a dividend of 2.2 percent, a number that had not varied in 31 years — never up, never down, always 2.2 percent. It was for that consistent income that most of its stockholders bought the shares — banks, pension funds, retired people. In 1950, the share price was 10. A decade later, it was 11 1/4.

The definition of sleepy.

And on the first day, Clarice bought 2,000 shares. This was a trade that no one would notice.

On the second day, 3,000 shares. On the third day, 5,000. On the fourth day, Clarice bought 10,000 shares. This was more shares than the stock normally traded in a week. Riom generally didn't move more than 1/8th of a point per day, either way, and maybe 1/2 of a point in a big week — usually because some pension fund needed to park some money in a safe place that still earned a little something. That week, Riom went up by 3/4 of a point. No one noticed.

The second week, Clarice did nothing. Riom fell back to where it had been before she started buying.

The third week, she bought another 20,000 over the course of five days. At the end of the week, Riom was up a full point. And if that was considered volatile, and if the volume was surging because of her purchases, again, there was no discernible reaction from any of the brokers with whom she interacted. No one in The Parquet said a word.

The fourth week, Clarice again did nothing. Riom fell back by 1/2 of a point.

The fifth week, 30,000.

The sixth week, nothing.

The seventh week, 50,000.

The eighth week, nothing.

Then, the ninth week, Clarice went all in. From Monday to Friday she bought 250,000 shares of Riom — 50,000 per day. By the end of the week, she had her full position: 370,000 shares at an average price of 13. It was almost the entire quarterly stake of the La Rue funds that she was managing, almost the full five million francs.

She had guessed about her ability to keep the price relatively stable while making such an enormous bet, and she had been correct. That is, as soon as the volatility grew because of her purchases, some of the pension funds and the conservative investors got scared and were happy to sell at a small profit and find another sleepy dividend payer. They liked making money, but too much, too soon? They found that frightening.

As a result, there were always shares available for Clarice to accumulate. She never had to chase the price — well, at least not too much.

And that was the Friday, the ninth Friday, with her entire position in place, that the other brokers finally noticed. Most had never considered Riom as a potential investment. One of them, François Durand — fat man, tight vest, red splotches on his face, one of the half-dozen drinks a night crowd — even said to her, "I hate to admit it, but I had to look up exactly what Riom did to make its money."

Durand was one of 10 brokers whom Clarice had needed to enlist in placing her orders in that final week. The positions had become too big to manage on her own. And the truth was that washerwomen had nothing over brokers when it came to gossip and whispers, and it probably took only a couple phone calls for all 10 of the brokers to recognize that Clarice was up to something. Which was how she had planned it.

"A hunch," is what she told all of the people at The Parquet who asked — and at least one time, she was talking to a crowd that was three deep around her stool.

"More silver? More lead?"

Clarice shook her head.

"A new vein? A new mining technique?"

Clarice put on a stone face that betrayed the smallest, quickest of smiles. She had practiced the look in the reflection from her medicine cabinet that morning, and again in her compact mirror just before coming over to the bar. She couldn't tell if she had pulled it off, not for sure, but she was pretty confident.

"A good value," is what she told all of them. "And if I'm wrong, I still have the dividend. I don't think it's risky at all. In fact, I think it's conservative."

15

Henri was the first to arrive at the Luxembourg Garden, which was the place where these kinds of meetings of the La Rue family took place. You know, the kinds of meetings where they discussed a gang war that had forced them into hiding. And if this one didn't exactly fit — it wasn't a potential war against all of them, only Martin — Gerard put the process into motion anyway. He got the phone call from Martin and contacted Henri and Michel.

They always met in the part of the Luxembourg Garden where the old men played chess — the old men and the young kids with greasy hair. Henri dragged four of the green metal chairs into a circle and waited. A genius invention, those chairs — too heavy to steal but just light enough to move around. The last time they had done this was when they had the problem with the Levines, but that was more than a year earlier. It had been quiet since.

Gerard and Lemieux arrived next, and the priest did the math and dragged a fifth chair into the circle. They were quiet for a minute, and then Gerard cleared his throat.

"Your fucking brother," Gerard said.

"Your fucking nephew," Henri said.

Michel and Martin arrived from different directions of the park, about 30 seconds apart. When Martin was seated, and before he could begin talking, Gerard said, "Jean?"

Lemieux looked at Gerard and then at Martin. He said, "Did you know who they were?"

"I do now," Martin said. He explained about the telephone call from the cop on his payroll.

"Garreaus. Jesus Christ. But you didn't know before?"

"They were meddling in La Rue family business. You more than anyone should realize that can't be allowed to stand unchallenged."

"There are challenges short of shotguns. Like, you know, conversation. Or going to old man Garreau. That is, if you had known the dead kid's name. I mean, didn't you even fucking ask?"

"I asked."

"And the answer?"

Martin shrugged. Then he said half to himself, "Family honor."

"Enough." It was Lemieux speaking and Gerard nodded almost imperceptibly. "Marie, she's safe?"

"Likely getting a facial at the George V as we speak. She's fine. Nobody knows."

"Maiden name?" Lemieux said.

Martin nodded.

Then the priest was quiet. He had been able to identify the problem but he wasn't prepared with a solution. He had not been born into this thing and he was out of his depth.

"I'm worried about Guy and Clarice," Henri said.

"It's my problem, not theirs," Martin said. It was as if the notion hadn't dawned on him.

"You killed a grandson. Guy and Clarice are of the same

generation in our family. Eye for an eye. Your problem is our problem, you fucking..."

"Enough." This time it was Gerard. "Clarice, not an issue. Guy can stay with Nico for a day or two. But I think, and I can't believe I'm saying this, that Martin is right. They came after him. They'll keep coming after him. I don't think the rest of us really have an issue."

He stopped. In the silence, Henri noticed the thwack-thwack-thwack from the nearby tennis courts.

"I'll handle it from here," Michel said.

The other four looked at him.

"I've hired some men from the 6th before, freelance," Michel said. "It's not that big a place. I can ask some questions, get some quick answers. I think I'm in a better position than any of the rest of you."

Lemieux said, "But if we kill another one..."

"Family honor," Martin said. His appearance was almost catatonic.

"Not kill, not necessarily," Michel said. "I get the information, and we deal with it. And if we have to give the Garreaus one or two of your shitty cafés to make the whole thing go away, so be it."

Gerard shrugged. Fine.

Henri, though, was intrigued. Maybe it was as simple as Michel had explained — that he had the connections, and that he might be able to settle things before they exploded — not that the Garreaus were capable of much of an explosion. As a family, they likely topped out at a weak fart.

Still, the whole Martin/Michel dynamic had seemed off for months, and this just added to it.

"Need any men?"

"I can handle it," Michel said.

"I can give you Freddy."

"No, I've got it."

"Best gun in the family."

"No, I can handle it," Michel said.

Henri eventually shrugged, as Gerard had. The last thing the old man said as they stood up was to Martin: "And you, you fucking stay in the George V until you hear different."

PART IV

16

Michel had hired a couple of freelancers out of the 6th arrondissement before, and the 6th really wasn't a big or complicated place in the mob sense. The truth was, the mob dynamic in Paris really wasn't very complicated anywhere in the city. Families had their spheres of influence and ruled them as they saw fit. Conflicts tended to happen when stupid people got greedy — not that often — or when, like two men seated next to each other on an airplane, their elbows kept banging on the armrest in between. This wasn't any armrest thing, though. This was a stupid thing.

Michel knew this, too, because he had already made his inquiries. It didn't take an hour, as it turned out. He discovered three things in a total of three phone calls. First, that the dead kid was, indeed, the grandson of Sylvain Garreau. Second, that old Sylvain was currently on vacation in Malaga along with his two top lieutenants and their wives. He didn't even know what had happened yet, mostly because no one had a phone number for the place where Sylvain was staying in Malaga. His people, junior people, were currently paralyzed as a result. And third, that the dead kid was, indeed, freelancing. They were pretty sure that his grandfather didn't know, and that there was no father (dead from cancer), and that the old man had pretty much washed his hands of the dead kid years earlier. As Michel's source said, "Greedy, drunk and maybe a homo — and with that, the old man was done."

Michel knew all of this before he volunteered to save Martin's ass. And while he couldn't predict exactly how the grandfather would react when he called in from the villa in Malaga, the best guess would be that the old man would order some kind of half-hearted retribution. Martin qualified for the retribution — as least, that was what Michel figured.

So, there were the four remainders from the dead kid's free-lance posse. They might be joined by some conventional Garreau soldiers after the phone call from Malaga, which was a complication Michel did not need. Or, and this was the bigger concern, the old man might find a way to get word to Gerard and arrange some kind of conference between gang old-timers to broker a solution.

Maybe there wouldn't need to be bloodshed. The kid was a waste, after all, and maybe a homo. Of all the possible outcomes, the peace treaty was the one Michel couldn't have.

Because the more he thought about it, the more he thought that now was the time to get rid of Martin in a permanent way.

He was such an idiot, even if he did have Michel's balls in his pocket — now and maybe forever. Such an idiot. It galled Michel whenever he thought about it. Whenever he thought about, well, pick an idiocy. Any idiocy would do. A favorite was the time, after a meeting in Gerard's house, when Martin had to rush out early and Henri told them why.

"A chick with a dick," Henri said.

The priest wasn't there. Michel burst out laughing. Gerard required an explanation. Michel laughed all the way through it. Gerard turned red.

"How do you know?"

"One of his guys," Henri said. "I pay him to, well, to keep tabs on my genius brother."

"So..."

"So, it happened. Picked her up in a bar, went back to her place. His. Whatever. Got all the way to the point where there was no disguising the realities. And, well, Martin freaked out."

"And your guy knows this how?"

"He's Martin's driver. He was waiting outside the apartment in the car. And, for what it's worth, he couldn't tell she wasn't a woman, either."

"Freaked out?" Michel said.

"A euphemism for 'beat her to death with an ashtray.'"

"Christ," Gerard said. He actually blessed himself.

"And the problem?" Michel said.

"Fingerprints on the ashtray," Henri said. "Oh, and running his mouth at the bar beforehand, the bar where he picked her up."

"Him."

"Whatever. But he was buying drinks for everyone, and they all knew his name, and the cops..."

"Stupid fucking..." This time, Gerard did not bless himself.

"Don't worry, don't worry, I worked it out," Henri said. He explained how he talked to Chrétien, his cop, who talked to the captain in the 7th, who talked to the detective working the case.

"It's going to cost him a ton of cash, but it'll be taken care of."

"And he was running off just now—"

"To pay the captain in the 7th," Henri said.

Martin did something like that every few months, almost without fail — not necessarily involving dead transvestites, just other things equally as stupid. Usually they were deals that turned out to be impossible schemes. Martin was like that, always trying to make a huge score and prove how smart he was, only to demonstrate again how naive and intellectually lazy he really was.

As Henri liked to say, "So many rainbows, so many pots of shit."

So why not let Martin get killed?

What was the downside?

Michel did a quick calculation. Because he had said he would take care of it, his prestige with Gerard and Henri would suffer if Martin didn't survive. Then again, so what? It wasn't as if they could do without Michel's expertise — and they sure as hell couldn't do without the heroin money. It was probably half of what they took in overall. As for Martin's income from the liquor business — they could replace him with a chimp and do as well. But the heroin smuggling? Michel had the expertise and, more importantly, the connections in Marseille. Those, the La Rue family couldn't replace.

The way Michel figured it, if he could work it out that Martin did something else stupid and got himself killed as a result, none of the blame would splatter onto his suit. And, well, even if he did get splattered, Gerard and Henri would let it go. After all, Martin really was an idiot.

17

Thursday evening, just getting dark, the lights in the houses surrounding Place des Vosges beginning to flick on, one by one. When Father Jean Lemieux sat there on one of the benches, sat there in civilian clothes, he thought that this was his favorite time of day in his favorite place in all of the world.

Not that he had seen much of it — Rome, Madrid, Frankfurt, fin. Oh, and cities around France. It was never for a vacation, though, always for a meeting of the men who did what he did in other European archdioceses. He'd never had the money for anything more than a week in a pension in Brittany.

Place des Vosges at twilight. There were still a couple of little kids running around with nannies yelling about the need to get home for dinner — but the shouts were half-hearted, drowned out by the happy shrieks of the children. Lemieux looked at the lit windows. A woman stepped into one of them, her husband behind her, the man fiddling with the buttons on the back of her dress. It fell down over one shoulder, and then she pulled down the blind. She looked like his mother, just a little. And then, like he was riffling through a stack of photographs, he saw her, eyes-wide screaming, and then her raised right hand, and then the bruise on his shoulder, or chest, or cheek — her aim varied — and then her return to his room after he was in his pajamas, and then the book she read him many times over. *The Calico Cat from Casablanca*. Even when it was new, it seemed to drawings were faded.

Lemieux thought about all of that, about the riffling photographs, and then he thought about the money he'd never had before but which he had now. So much money. It was all that was on his mind as he began the walk, the lefts and the rights through the alleys, the turns made automatically, without thinking. Left, left, right, left — so much money. Two more years — that was all he would need. And then, well, he could live like a prince. Really, truly, a prince.

When he got to the door, Lemieux was greeted like the regular customer he was. Yes, Patrice was available. Yes, come right in.

There were times when he thought Patrice merely went through the motions, but this night was not one of those. The slaps — on his face, on his ass — were crisp. The insults, the degradation — they, too, were on point:

"It gets smaller every time, you goddamn baby..."

"You weak, pathetic piece of shit..."

"Don't you dare fucking cry..."

Later, after he was dressed and having a drink in the bar, he felt the breast pocket of his sport coat. The passport was there — the new false passport in the name of Claude Ransom. It had cost a lot but, then again, not really. His share of the La Rue money was beyond what he had imagined when the whole scheme began to move. Just two years more — that's all he would need, all he would ever need. Two years, and maybe even quicker if he was willing to fiddle with the books. He knew the places in the house where Gerard stashed his money, and if he could help himself and then adjust the ledger...

He thought about it, but maybe not. Why risk it? Two years would be fine. Two years and he would be a prince. Maybe in Casablanca, in Morocco.

18

Fast Frankie, for some reason, had continued to keep in touch with and do business with Clarice. The fact that her father had beaten the shit out of him, intimidated him into running parallel nefarious schemes for Henri and Clarice — and coming within an inch of losing his seat on the bourse — seemed to have been no deterrent. He had been the one who made the business approaches, too. He had been the one to call with the lunch invitation.

Fast Frankie was François Delhomme, and the nickname was the result of his tendency to play along the edges of what was acceptable business practice for the men who held seats on the bourse. There weren't that many of them, and their money was old, and they had standards. The curb brokers worked around the margins more because they had no choice if they were to survive. But the men with seats, most held in their families for generations, could still rake in the cash while maintaining their moral rectitude.

Fast Frankie was different, though. He had inherited the seat, and his family never had the wealth of the others, and he needed to push the envelope. The need was financial but also, well, it fit his personality. As he said, "They can shove their moral rectitude up their rectums, although the sticks that are already up there might make things a tad uncomfortable."

Fast Frankie had assisted Clarice with an insider transaction that wasn't illegal, not exactly, but that was frowned upon. He didn't want to do it, and only agreed after Henri broke his nose and threatened worse — and the thing was, as Clarice has told him, they would never get caught for that. It was the other thing, Henri's thing: framing an art dealer in a securities scam that would get the art dealer on the front of *France-Soir* in handcuffs. And if the art dealer never went to jail — hung jury — it didn't matter. The embarrassing picture was enough for Henri's audience of one: his wife Sylvie, who happened to be sleeping with the art dealer at the time.

Anyway, Frankie blamed the art dealer's deceit, the art dealer claimed it was fiction, and the overseers at the bourse — like the jury in the trial — didn't know how to sort it out. So they went with the tried and true, a stern warning and a lecture on moral rectitude.

"Moral rectitude, my rectum," Frankie said at lunch that day. He retold her a variation of the story every time he had a second drink, and she laughed in all of the appropriate places. Why he hadn't run and hid from her after he'd been forced to walk around for weeks with foundation on his face to cover the bruises, Clarice had no idea. But he hadn't run, and he could still have his uses.

It was in the middle of the third drink when he got to the point of the lunch, something she well knew ahead of time. She had been determined not to bring it up herself, though. As she had practiced variations of the conversation in her head, she always thought it best that Frankie go first. Which he did, after his first sip of his third martini.

"Riom," he said. "Or, rather, boring-ass, not-worth-a-second-look Riom. What exactly are you up to?"

"A hunch," she said.

"A hunch, my ass. I mean, what the hell?"

"Really, just a feeling. And I'll take the dividend in the meantime and see if I'm right. If I'm wrong, fuck it, I'll sell it at a small profit. There's no risk."

"There's a lost opportunity cost, and you know it," Frankie said. "I've felt the business end of your father's elbow. I know the La Rues a little better than I might have a couple of years ago. And there is nothing about your family that suggests they would be happy with a 2.2 percent dividend."

"As a part of a bigger portfolio—"

"My ass," Frankie said. He liked to say "my ass," it seemed. Clarice smiled as she considered it. Maybe it was Freudian. Or, maybe it was just the martinis.

"Listen, Frankie—"

"There is no way in hell that 2.2 percent is anything close to what you, a La Rue, are expecting out of this investment. You're not the goddamned School Teachers' Old Age Pension Fund. I mean, Christ, you insult my intelligence."

"Come on, Frankie—"

"And you hurt me, too. I mean, why didn't you involve me? You used a bunch of people, including that fat fuck Durand, but not me."

"Do you know that you're Fast Frankie and he's Fat Frankie?"

"Whatever," François Delhomme said. "Stop changing the subject. What gives?"

"I'm telling you, a hunch hedged by the dividend."

"Bullshit. Who's your insider?"

"Nobody. That's the truth."

"So, that's the truth but the hunch part is bullshit."

"That's not what I said."

"Jesus Christ."

"It's a good company with a good value that pays a dividend—"

"That pays a dividend that your father couldn't be bothered to wipe his ass with," Frankie said.

Clarice smiled, just the once. It had been part of her plan. Just the once. And even as Frankie badgered her through the main course, she stuck to the story and to the sincerity. No more smiles. Just the once.

Then, the next day, the share price of The Riom Mining Company had increased by a half-point. Besides the usual trading, there had been a single order of 50,000 shares. It had been Fast Frankie, without question. The price was now 16. Her gain, if she were to sell, would be 23 percent.

19

Celeste did not know what Gerard did, what his family did. She lived over in the 12th, far enough away. And the La Rues of 1917 were not the La Rues of 1960, not nearly — smaller, less wealthy, less established, less polished. Mostly smaller. He was pretty sure their name had never been in the newspapers, not for anything other than marriages and obituaries.

He had met her at a dance hall over in Montparnasse. She was there with a group of friends, and he was there with Big Jean and a few others on the La Rue payroll. They had been thrown together during a line dance — the dance involved a whip where, on each rotation around the floor, the end of the male line was released into the arms of the end of the female line. He would tell her, weeks later, "Imagine if I hadn't changed places with Big Jean when he stumbled."

"Fate, then," she said.

The truth was that he had pushed Big Jean out of the way. He had noticed her on the line minutes earlier and fixed the order. Fate was for saps and for women, Gerard believed.

They were in the Tuileries, sitting in two of the chairs

arrayed around the Bassin Octogonol. The fountain in the middle was dancing, and Place de la Concorde was in the distance behind it. The sun was bright, and Celeste's eyes were closed. It was three months after that night in the dance hall, about six weeks after the other thing. His call-up notice was still several weeks away. The sun felt so warm. He held Celeste's hand and closed his eyes, too. The day was perfect.

The other thing. Gerard almost never thought about it, but he did that day. The truth was that, the morning after — the very next morning — it was gone from his consciousness. But that day, for whatever reason, he was replaying the night in his head. Maybe it was the sun. Maybe the feeling of complete relaxation had robbed his unconscious of its guardians. Whatever.

The other thing. Celeste had a boyfriend of long standing on the night they met in the dance hall. Paul. Gerard never knew the last name. He only knew about Paul because one of her friends told him — warned him, more like. She was drunk, and Celeste was on the floor with her other friends, and Genevieve spilled it all while simultaneously spilling her beer. Paul. Boyfriend. "Almost her fiancé," Genevieve said, stumbling over the f.

It was at the same dance hall, two weeks later. Paul, apparently, didn't like to dance. What he liked to do was drink with his buddies at The Squawking Parrot. And what he looked like, well, Genevieve said, "A giant, 6-foot-5, with black hair that looked as if it had been cut with hedge clippers." She stumbled over the p's, and just the slightest spray of spittle caught Gerard's cheek.

He had not been yet been alone with Celeste on a proper date, and wouldn't be that night, either, not with Genevieve and the rest of her friends at the dance hall. So he made up a work excuse and told her he had to get home early. But instead of heading back up the butte, he drove to the corner of Rue Louis Braille and Rue de Toul, to The Squawking Parrot.

He parked his car across the street, a half-block down. He got out, removed his license plate with a screwdriver he kept in the glove box, got back in, and waited. It wasn't an hour, closer to a half-hour, when the big man with black hair came out of the bar. He was with two friends, and they stood beneath the sign with the toucan on it and smoked a cigarette. As he watched, all he could think about was how correct Genevieve had been. Even from a half-block away, the wild nest of black hair perched on Paul's was his most distinctive feature, even more than his height.

They finished their cigarettes and began to walk. Stumble, really — and Paul more than the others. The friends turned in Gerard's direction, Paul in the opposite direction — so he needed to pull away from the curb and make a U-turn. It was easy enough. There was no traffic on the street.

When he got himself turned, Gerard drove slowly, school-zone slowly, even less. As he watched, he saw that Paul was using the entire sidewalk as he maneuvered — that's how drunk he was. He actually collided with an apartment building within 30 seconds — collided and bounced off, and then it was all inertia but in the opposite direction. He nearly tripped into the gutter on the rebound but managed to stop himself at the very edge of the curb — stop himself, teetering. Into the street? On the sidewalk? You could have gotten odds on the gutter, but Paul somehow stayed perched on the curb. His last victory.

Then, after regaining his balance, Paul stopped on the second corner he came to, set his feet wide, and began to piss on a garbage can. It took him about 10 seconds to undo his fly, but he managed eventually. Head down, concentrating on his business, Paul never saw the car. He might have heard the acceleration because Gerard floored it, but Paul never looked up from the act of admiring his stream. Gerard remembered that much, but tended not to think about the rest, especially the part where he reversed over the body just to make sure.

But he was thinking about it that day in the Tuileries, eyes closed, face warmed by the sun. Celeste squeezed his hand, and he squeezed back. It all felt perfect. Magical. Fated.

She squeezed his hand again. Saps and women, then. Saps and women.

PART V

20

Michel knew he couldn't approach the four knuckleheads directly — too dangerous and, besides, not nearly elegant enough for his taste. Michel took pride in his business, and disliked the blunt instrument as a weapon. Oh, sometimes you didn't have a choice, but this was not one of those times. A little subtlety would work here, he knew. There was no need for a two-by-four between the eyes.

And so, Michel had worked out what he considered to be a nice little two-cushion bank shot. It would take only two nights to accomplish, and the only danger would be to his liver.

The first night, he parked himself at a back corner table in The Leaping Frog, an ancient café in the 6th known to one and all as The Frog — and known also for the perpetual stickiness of the floor. Michel sometimes wondered how often they washed it, and if it felt any cleaner on those days. He didn't think so. Every time he had been there — easily two dozen times — he had found himself doing the same thing after he sat down, doing it again and again. That is, setting his foot completely flat on the floor and then appreciating the resistance he felt as he lifted it, the resistance and the tiny sound to sole and floor coming apart. A whispered *thwock*.

The drinks at The Frog were cheap, and the clientele tended to be made up less of amateur drinkers than of seasoned professionals. It was a café where the food was no more than passable, which was fine, seeing as how almost nobody arrived with the idea of eating anything more complicated than a Croque Monsieur. It was dim and dirty and more than fine for people of certain proclivities. Gulp, bang down the glass on the scarred wooden tables, another. *Thwock*.

The Frog was where Philippe Houle finished most of his evenings. He was a soldier for hire, and Michel sometimes wondered how guys like Philippe made ends meet. It wasn't as if Paris mob families often needed outside assistance — they tended to have too many men on the payroll as it was. Michel certainly felt that way about the La Rues. He couldn't believe how the brothels were staffed, especially Trinity One. And what for? How many 25-year-old lunkheads does it take to throw out the occasional drunk?

But Michel knew Philippe Houle because he had used him twice during smuggling operations, just as security. Philippe never pulled a gun for him, never did anything more dangerous than follow a truck delivering product along the distribution route. Still, they had a relationship, and Philippe's face lit up when he saw Michel sitting alone at the back table. The way Michel figured it, Philippe was happy because he assumed — correctly — that Michel would be buying.

What Philippe did not know, and would not be told, was that Michel had been tipped by one of his other contacts that Philippe had been contracted by the late Jean Garreau and his band of four young dopes. And, likely for the cost of a night's drinks — perhaps consumed at the very same table where they were now sitting — Philippe had provided a list of a few of the

La Rue-controlled cafés and bars in the 6th as well as a helpful map of their locations.

So, Michel toyed with him. He said, "Those fucking Garreau animals," and Philippe nodded in agreement.

"My cousin, he had nothing to do with it."

Another nod in reply.

"Even if he did, they fucking deserved what they got — the fucking nerve. There are rules here, after all."

Another nod.

"Him and his wife, for them to have to hide—"

"Disgraceful, absolutely disgraceful," Philippe said.

"I mean, prisoners in their own city—"

"Disgraceful."

That was the only reply Philippe could come up with — "disgraceful." He was pretty drunk already, Michel figured. But even in that state, Michel was fairly sure the key point had registered. He said it one more time, a few minutes later, just to be sure:

"Prisoners in their own city."

Then they had one more drink and spent the last few minutes decrying the decline of standards in their world. Michel's side of the conversation was complete bullshit, as he would prefer to dismantle the whole mob family structure. He saw it as flabby and expensive and unnecessary in 1960. But, well, whatever.

That done, Michel headed to a decidedly more upscale place over in the 8th the next night. It was a dance club just off the Champs, not far from the Lido. The Octagon. Michel didn't go for the dancing, though. He was there an hour before opening, when the bartenders arrived for their shifts. One bartender in particular, Bertrand Mimieux.

While Michel wasn't in the retail sales business, he did always manage to shave small quantities of heroin from large shipments and keep it for strategic purposes. Bert the bartender at The Octagon was one such purpose. Michel supplied him at a more than fair price, and Bert offered information in return. Nothing big — just what important people might be at the club, and if he heard anything interesting about other mob families or about heroin in general. And if it had never paid off in anything much above the level of gossip, this would be different.

Because if Philippe Houle liked The Frog, and the cheap drinks, and the *thwock,* his twin brother Reginald liked nice suits and perfume in the air and the musical stylings of The First Estate, the eight-piece house band at The Octagon. Philippe and Reginald could not be more different, other than that they emerged from the same womb on the same day and chose the freelance mob soldier business as their profession.

Reginald had worked for Michel, too, on the same jobs running security as his brother. Michel had noticed the dynamic between the twins. Philippe was older by a few minutes but he acted like it was a few years. It was like Henri and Martin — the serious older brother talking down to the flighty younger brother, and the flighty younger brother always trying to prove that he was smarter than the serious older brother.

On this night, Michel and Reginald would not speak — Michel would be gone before The Octagon opened. Delivering the message would be Bert's job. In exchange for a small envelope — there would be no financial charge — Bert would be required to whisper one fact to Reginald in as conspiratorial a manner as he could.

One fact: "You'll never believe who I saw going into the George V this afternoon. Martin Fucking La Rue. Isn't he supposed to be hiding out?"

That would do it. The way Michel calculated it, Reginald would tell Philippe the next day in an attempt to demonstrate the superiority of his knowledge over his older brother. And the day after that, two days at the most, Philippe would connect his brother's tidbit with Michel's words — "Prisoners in their own city" — and find a way to get word to the four knuckleheads who worked for the departed Jean Garreau. He would do it for drinks, probably. He might even draw them a map.

A two-cushion bank shot, then. Elegant.

21

Henri was in his office in the back of the uniform store, door closed, thinking. How long would Martin need to stay in the George V? How long would it take Michel to eliminate the problem? And why was he really worried about it, other than that it was a business complication? It wasn't as if Martin hadn't brought the whole damn thing down on himself.

He was wondering, figuring that Martin and Marie would be eating room service for at least a week, probably. And, well, whatever. A week, maybe 10 days. Michel had made it his problem, for whatever reason, and Henri had no intention of getting any more involved. That's what he kept telling himself, anyway. He was almost at the point of believing it, too — that he could fight the urge to control the situation — when his thoughts were interrupted by a knock on the office door. The receptionist handed him a note.

"The guy didn't want to talk to you, just this," she said.

He read the note:

"Mr. Brown, urgent."

He couldn't remember the last time he had received an

"urgent." His first thought was Martin. He called the George V and was put through to the room immediately. Martin and Marie were having the coq au vin, and he could hear Marie bitching that it was getting cold. If they were still alive, what could be so urgent?

Henri had one of Passy's guys drive him over to the park on Rue Burq — well, two blocks away. When he entered, there was no one in the back, no kids, no moms, no nannies. But Chrétien was there, pacing on the dirt patch that would have been perfect for boules.

"What?"

"Sit down."

"What?"

"It's a long story," Chrétien said. And then he told it. One of Freddy's guys was dead, found in bed with a woman whose husband had made the unfortunate decision to surprise her at lunchtime. As soon as Chrétien said that part, his breath caught.

"Where?"

"Over in the 17th, by the Square des Batignolles."

At which point, Henri's head dropped.

"Dead woman is Gillian Merced."

"Wife of?"

"Yes, wife of. Dead guy in the bed with her is one Robert Lefranc. Age 25. Yours?"

Henri nodded. "One of Freddy's."

This was not the whole story, Henri knew. Dead young men were found in dead older women's beds every day in Paris. Well, every week, anyway. It was commonplace. The only time the story would get big play in *France-Soir* was when the husband was found at the scene with a gun in his hand, screaming about betrayal and vindication. The picture of the husband being taken away in handcuffs, walking down the front steps of the apartment house, was a timeless classic. The husband. It was always the husband.

This one would get the front-page treatment even without the photo, though. Dead wife of a police captain, dead sap in the bed — yes, that kind of story would play. Even if Robert Lefranc was identified as a La Rue soldier, though, it seemed survivable.

Why urgent?

"Captain Rodrique Merced was also found at the scene," Chrétien said. "He hanged himself."

Still not urgent, Henri thought. Better newspaper story but still not urgent. Still not.

"He was hanging from a drain pipe, with the note he had written stuffed into his shirt pocket."

And there it was.

Urgent.

Oh, shit.

"He lays out the whole thing in the note," Chrétien said. "Very honest, our crooked Captain Merced. He talks about how he was on your payroll, and how he looked the other way when the La Rues had their way with shipments arriving at the Gare du Nord, and how he tried to squeeze you for more, and how you sent the unfortunate Mr. Lefranc to bed his wife in order the squeeze him, and how you took pictures."

"It was Freddy."

"A distinction without a difference, Henri."

"Yes."

Henri thought for a second while Chrétien took a breath. Very bad, no doubt. But there had to be options. As long as there were corrupt policemen, as long as there was French currency in multiple denominations, there had to be options.

"I have the note," Chrétien said. "You can relax about that."

"Have it?"

"Burned it in my wastebasket at the precinct. It's going to

cost you a shitload, but I did get it. Only the one detective, the one who arrived at the scene first, found it and saw it. He's a good guy, amenable. He's been around the block and was happy to have a conversation. And, like I said. A shitload."

"Not a problem, then," Henri said.

"No, still one more problem."

"What?"

"The esteemed and aggrieved Captain Rodrique Merced."

"What about him?"

"He didn't die."

"You said he hanged himself."

"Which he did. He did indeed. He yanked the cord out of a lamp in the bedroom and tied it around his neck and stepped off of a chair, just like in the movies. He did hang himself, though ineptly. He survived. He was unconscious at the scene, barely breathing but, indeed, breathing. As we speak, he is still breathing and still unconscious in a room at St. Clare's."

"Prognosis?"

Chrétien looked at his watch.

"Not dead as of about 25 minutes ago. Not dead is all I have for you."

22

When you were in the uniform supply business, you were in the uniform supply fraternity. It was a loose confederation, granted, but it was not unheard of for the nurse's uniform supply company to take on a little extra sewing work in August from the La Rue school uniform company, right before schools opened. It wasn't unusual for the doormen's uniform company to obtain some needed buttons from the police uniform company, and the like. They all met every year for a drink in the Hotel Lutèce and swapped stories about the price of cotton fabric, a laugh riot. But it was how Henri knew that the clergy uniform supply store was close to the park, on Rue Berthe, and it was how he could get away with telling the owner how he needed to borrow a cassock for a few hours for a prank he was pulling on an old friend. And it was how the owner, whom he only knew as Salvy, agreed to give him a threadbare cassock and a beat-up old biretta that a priest had left behind after getting a new outfit. The cassock was a little snug, but fine. The biretta fit perfectly.

"When you come back for your clothes, you tell me the whole story," Salvy said.

"Just a few hours," Henri said.

He took the Metro six stops and walked the five blocks to St. Clare's. It was unlike him to act so impulsively, but there wasn't time for planning or consultation. He liked to think he was prudent, not necessarily cautious — and the prudent thing was to act with haste and to act alone. He didn't want Gerard or that fucking Father Lemieux to know about how he had used his leverage against Captain Merced after claiming that there was no leverage to use, and how he had pocketed the extra cash that he said Merced had squeezed from him. That was the big thing — but the other was the time pressure. If Merced woke up and began blabbing, there was no telling how big *France-Soir* would make the story. And if he would be embarrassed if Gerard found out he had been shorting the envelope, the consequences of a full-blown public discussion of police payoffs at the train stations would be, well, untidy. It just wouldn't do.

The way Henri figured it, nobody would look twice at a priest in a hospital. A doctor or nurse might be better, but the risks there were obvious. Priest was better. The halls were likely crawling with them.

Merced's room was on the third floor. It was a double room, but the other bed was empty and a curtain was pulled across between them. Two old women were at Merced's bedside when Henri walked in.

"Oh, Father," the one woman said, and the two of them blessed themselves. They were both 70 if they were a day. Mother, aunts, something like that. After a minute, introductions were made. Two aunts, it turned out. The mother had been there but left to meet the children at home when they returned from school.

"She thought she should be the one," the talkative aunt said. The other just stared into space and mumbled and worked the rosary beads she held in front of her waist.

"The doctors?" Henri said.

"Not optimistic," the talkative aunt said. "Potential for brain damage, he said. But he would know more when Rodrique wakes up."

Pause.

"If he wakes up," she said, and then the one with the rosary beads sobbed.

"Poor man," Henri said. He chose to ignore the fact that the church wanted nothing to do with people who killed themselves. The parish priest would likely deal with that later.

"The doctor was just here," the talkative aunt said. "He told us he would be back in an hour to see."

Pause.

"To see if he wakes up," she said, and the other one sobbed again.

"I'd like to pray with your nephew alone for a few minutes, if I could," Henri said. "A private time, an important time. Just 10 or 15 minutes, no more — but it is something I have done in the past, and it is very meaningful to me, and I believe it will be meaningful to God and to your nephew, whatever is to come."

The two aunts looked at each other.

"Ten minutes, really," Henri said. He pulled out a few coins. "Let the church buy you a cup of coffee. It's going to be a long day and night, I think."

The two old ladies agreed and left the room. Henri closed the door behind them and checked his watch. He needed to be in and out in 10 minutes. He opened the drawer in the little bureau next to the bed and pulled out the prop he had hoped to find — a Bible. Old Testament in the front, New Testament in the back, he decided on the New Testament and picked a random page. Book of Matthew. Whatever.

He stood next to the bed and leaned over. Merced's

breathing was so shallow that he had to put his ear right next to the thieving cop's lips to hear it.

Henri placed the Bible next to Merced's pillow and leaned over the barely-alive body. With his left hand, he pinched Merced's nostrils closed. With his forearm, he covered Merced's mouth. How long it might take, he had no idea. It was about two minutes by his watch when the door opened behind him. He was startled, and knocked the Bible on the floor.

"Oh, so sorry, Father," the nurse said.

"A particularly moving passage from Matthew — I was whispering it in his ear," Henri said. "Well, I was moved by it, transfixed by it, and you startled me. Am I in your way?"

She looked at Merced.

"He's still—"

"Breathing, yes," Henri said. "But barely. I sent his aunts down for a coffee so I could have some private time with this poor soul. You know, before..."

"Don't you use oils for the anointing?"

"Yes, but this is different. A small prayer service I have developed for, well, for these times. The extreme unction will be later."

The nurse nodded and withdrew. Henri looked at his watch. Four minutes.

He went back to the business of killing Merced — nose pinched, mouth covered. Henri didn't know if the cop had been sedated, but he didn't struggle in any way. His eyes never opened. He got a little bit blue, but maybe not. The light in the room was dim.

There were no machines in the room. Merced wasn't hooked up to anything. That was good and bad — good because an alarm wouldn't be tripped if the breathing or the heart ceased, bad because Henri really couldn't tell if he was succeeding.

Henri looked at his watch again. Down to a minute. He

released the grip on Merced's nose and mouth and leaned down to listen. Nothing. He felt for a pulse. Nothing. It wasn't definitive but it was the best he could do. Even if he hadn't killed him, well, that was five or six more minutes in which the brain received no oxygen. There was no way to be sure, but Merced had to be existing somewhere on a scale between dead and vegetable.

Henri left the hospital room and took the back stairs. In, out, and no one looked twice. He didn't stop worrying until two hours later, though, when a phone call to the nursing supervisor at St. Clare's revealed that Captain Rodrique Merced, a thieving cop and a poor bastard, had died.

23

It was the next night, Friday night, and Henri and Sylvie were getting dressed to go out. Not with each other, though — Saturday nights were the wives' nights. Friday nights were for the girlfriends. It had been that way since at least Henri's grandfather, and it was understood by everyone involved before the exchange of vows. The wives didn't have to like it but they knew the deal. And part of the deal was that the subject really wasn't discussed except during the worst arguments between husband and wife — and even then, it wasn't an argument about who didn't love whom anymore, or about anything sexual. Once a year or so — and the men all knew this because they exchanged information — the wives seemed to need to bitch about how much money the husband was spending on the girlfriend. And if everyone on both sides of the argument knew that money was a catch-all for all the rest of their marital issues, a fight about money remained an acceptable way for the wives to blow off steam.

Or, as Freddy said the other month, "Well, it was my turn. And you know what? You shove a couple of new dresses down her throat and she fucking shuts up, just like that."

Henri was putting on a suit. Sylvie was getting into slacks and a sweater. The men and their girlfriends were going to the Moulin Rouge, which Henri hated — but it was part of the regular nightclub rotation. Sylvie was going over to Passy's apartment to play cards with the other wives. It had been months since Lucien Richard was arrested, but the malaise that enveloped Sylvie in the days after the news was splashed on the front of *France-Soir* had barely lifted. She spent her days in an uncomfortable emotional state, one that was somewhere north of miserable but somewhere south of contented. They had sex weekly-ish, but it was purely mechanical. Henri didn't know what to do about it other than to hope that time would heal.

They were two people short of their normal contingent at Moulin Rouge, given that Martin was still holed up in the George V. It had been a week. When Michel walked in with his latest — he was in his mid-thirties, a decade younger than Henri, and the girl looked like she was 20, younger than Clarice — Henri said, "Anything?"

"Getting there."

"Meaning?"

"Meaning, I'm getting there," Michel said. At which point, he turned away from Henri and led the girl to the table — or, rather, steered her with his right hand on her left butt cheek.

When they went to the Lido, which Henri much preferred — as he liked to say, "They have the classiest ass" — the men had a standing bet about who could be the first one to spot a stray pubic hair on one of the girls. Nobody had ever won. At the Moulin Rouge, the bet was about spotting a mole on one of the dancers' asses. That one was won about twice a year. Martin won the previous month, but it had been controversial. Freddy thought the mole was on the redhead's thigh, not her ass.

"Same thing," Martin said.

"Same thing, my ass," Freddy said.

"Her ass," Martin said.

"If it doesn't jiggle when you smack it, it's not her ass," Freddy said.

This went on for about five minutes before a poll among the men was taken. As it turned out, Michel cast the deciding vote — in favor of Martin. He said, "The most profound thing I can state is, the ass is in the eye of the beholder."

And while everyone laughed at the mock profundity, all Henri could think about was how Michel had supported Martin again, however trivial the issue.

Anyway, that night, no moles were spotted on thighs or asses or anywhere. As most other nights, the table rearranged itself during the evening — girls in front by the stage, men in the back.

Two jugglers were on the stage, tossing balls back and forth over the head of a bare-breasted redhead. Henri leaned over to Passy and smiled a dirty smile and said, "You and Renée — talk about asses. You'd better watch your fucking heart."

"Bah. I'm not fucking her anymore. Doc says I can't. She jerks me off sometimes, but that's it."

"That's a shame."

"She seems happier, I think," Passy said. "The bitch."

"So, why don't you—"

"Too old to change, Henri. I don't see how you do it."

Henri's girlfriend, name of Polly, was a new one. He needed to change every other year, give or take. The even years. Polly was Miss 1960, and they were in the uber-expensive first few months. If he had to sit through one more fitting at Dior, he was going to need to take on a part-time job.

Henri looked around. It was normally six couples — Henri, Passy, Timmy, Freddy, Martin and Michel, along with their current girlfriends. It was only five couples on Saturdays because Timmy wasn't married anymore. As he liked to say, "For you guys, it's wives on Saturday. For me, it's research and development on Saturday. And penicillin on Monday."

Guy had not reached the echelon where he would be invited to join, although his temporary assignment at Trinity One had edged him closer. Henri didn't think his son would want to come — he knew about the Friday nights and the girlfriends, but knowing was one thing and peeking down the front of the Dior of the woman your father was screwing on the side was another.

"Guy, how's he doing?"

"Good, good."

"You can tell me the truth."

"I am telling you the truth," Passy said. "The boys say he's been a good boss on the night-to-night. Money has been steady, maybe up a hair."

"Well, you keep an eye on him. No, lean on him."

"I am, I am."

The truth was, Passy was checking on Guy maybe three times a week, and most of it was just a breezy social call. The older man had checked out.

24

"What is this shit?" Gerard said.

"What shit?" Henri said

"The newspaper."

Henri knew the shit of which his uncle spoke, of course. The story was on the front of *France-Soir*, but without the picture of the perp on the front steps of the apartment building, it lacked the possible impact. More a jab than a roundhouse right. The story was beneath a one-column headline, with a headshot of Captain Rodrique Merced. It was a relatively restrained account of what had happened, and it mentioned Freddy's dead soldier in the fourth paragraph. He was not identified as a La Rue family employee, but Gerard still knew the name, Robert Lefranc. Henri had hoped it might get past him, but the old man still read the papers pretty closely.

"Killed by his dick, what can I say?"

"Listen, Henri—"

"Here's what happened. I had Freddy send a couple of his guys around when Merced started squeezing us, just to get a sense of who we were dealing with. It didn't lead to anything other than a picture of his wife and kids and the apartment building — really, nothing worthwhile. The best Freddy can figure it, his guy met the wife and let his hormones get the best of him."

Gerard didn't answer for maybe 15 seconds and then kind of harrumphed. The phone call ended 15 seconds after that, after Gerard said, "Well, maybe you can get the new cop at Gare du Nord for a cheaper price."

25

Sylvie dressed in what she considered to be her best serious attire, a midnight blue wool suit with a matching pillbox hat. She hadn't worn it in six months, the last time she had been to a funeral. Henri was gone, gone to wherever, doing whatever he did. And if he had business that day, so did she. Serious business.

Because even if she had no proof, she also had no doubt, none at all, that Henri had orchestrated the arrest of Lucien Richard.

He had made her feel young, Lucien had. He had made her feel vibrant and happy. He had been the first serious relationship she'd had outside of her marriage — twice a year with the butcher didn't count, she figured. And if Henri could have a girlfriend at all times, and a new one every other year, he had no right to object to Lucien Richard. Henri had no right to object and he clearly had no right to get Lucien somehow tied up in a bogus investment scheme that ended with Lucien wearing handcuffs on the front page of *France-Soir*.

And she knew it. She knew it almost immediately, knew it from the look on his face when he saw the newspaper lying there on the kitchen table that night. Right then, she could tell. What convinced her, though, was that he never asked her what was wrong in the days thereafter. She had been devastated, and she knew that it showed, but Henri never said anything. He just offered an unusual level of tender understanding when they were together, which wasn't that often. From the day of the newspaper story — and for weeks after that — Henri steered an abnormally wide berth from his wife. There were none of the spontaneous midweek lunches that had been their norm, and there were an unusual number of business dinners, too.

She considered confronting him. She thought about moving to the summer house in Normandy for a while. She didn't know what to do, not until she saw the crumpled invoice in his jacket pocket, the invoice from Chanel. The number on it astounded her. She never bought directly from the designers, always from Galeries Lafayette. She didn't spend half of that on her own outfits. She almost never spent more than a third of that.

She flattened out the invoice and put it in the drawer of her makeup table. Every night for a week, she had looked at it between daubs of cold cream. For 28 years she had put up with the girlfriends because it had been understood that she had to put up with it if she was to marry into the La Rue family. Back then, her mother had been the one to tell her. It was a one-stop shop for marital advice: the sex talk and the La Rue mistress talk, all in one dinner.

At one point — and Sylvie would never forget this — her mother said, "Not for everyone, but still..."

The last two words just hung there between them, the "but still..." It was her mother telling her that, in the grand scheme of things, there were worse arrangements than the one that all La Rue men insisted upon. What neither of them talked about, but what both of them understood, was the monetary salve that would go a long way toward healing any emotional wounds.

Sylvie agreed to the bargain and barely bitched about it — just a couple of times in all of those years. She barely bitched and, finally, with Lucien Richard, all she sought was an ounce of understanding on Henri's part. She never threw it in his face, and how Henri knew about Lucien remained a mystery to her. She had been quiet and discreet, and all she hoped for was that her cheating dog of a husband would afford her just a tiny measure of courtesy in return. A tiny measure. A speck, nothing more.

She opened the drawer of the makeup table and looked at the Chanel invoice again. Then she closed it, and applied a final bit of powder to her forehead. The appointment with the attorney was in a half-hour.

26

Sometimes Henri did business in his office at the uniform company. Other times he held his meetings over lunch at Gartner's, the restaurant around the corner. Guy was getting the lunch treatment that day. It was the normal meeting, Guy arriving with an envelope for his father, and his father checking up on the brothels and, now, the Trinity One casino.

Henri was stabbing at one of the eggs in his Salad Niçoise when Guy sat down.

"I thought you didn't get the eggs."

"So sue me, I'm hungry."

They did the envelope/business conversation in about 10 minutes. His father asked him about three different ways how involved Passy was, and Guy said about three different ways that they were in daily communication. Of course, it was less than that — but Henri wasn't going to find out from Guy.

At the end, they were having coffee. After stirring in the sugar, the father looked up at the son and said, "That fucking priest worries me."

It came out of nowhere, and it took a second for it to click in his head, that his father was talking about the Rev. Jean Lemieux.

"Worries you how?"

"I'm not sure. It's just a feeling — but, really, I guess it's more than that. Lemieux is a fucking problem."

"But—"

"It's like this," Henri said. "On the one hand, I don't have a reason — yet — to question any of the advice he's giving to Gerard. And part of me is honestly glad that somebody else is living in the house with him. It's a big place for an old man, alone. You know what I mean?"

"He could get a live-in housekeeper and bang her on the side, like normal old men."

"Christ, do you spend all of your free time dreaming about Gerard's sex life? I'm starting to worry about you."

Guy snorted.

Henri said, "But, well, if you think about it for five minutes, you can see that the possibilities for bullshit and mischief are real. And besides, there's the money."

"What money?"

"You don't think the good reverend is doing it for fucking free, do you?"

"How much?"

"Not your affair."

"Yet I'm asking anyway," Guy said.

Henri thought about it and just told him. He had laid out the split once before for Guy, when he'd first brought him into the business. But this was different with Lemieux, and he explained the new financial realities.

"So — wait a minute — that motherfucker is taking in 2 percent of everything and 12 percent of the pot and shoving it down his cassock? All of that for fucking holding Gerard's dick while he pisses, among other things"

"You and Gerard's dick. I told you there was that girl from the war. And now there's proof... On that matter, how is Nico?"

"Fine."

"No problems?"

"Good at work? Keeping him happy after work?"

"Yes and yes," Guy said. "But back to, I mean, honestly, 2 percent plus? Whose idea was it? Uncle's?"

"So he said."

"And you all agreed to that?"

"I objected. But it's not a democracy."

"Whatever. Don't priests take a vow of poverty?"

"I think that's nuns and monks," Henri said. "But, well, in any case, not this one."

Guy sipped his coffee and smiled. This was a level of La Rue family/business gossip to which he had never been privy. His father knew he was handling all of it — the Trinity One casino, the brothels, babysitting Nico — and making it look easy. And if he was exhausted all the time, and so busy that he had no chance of finding a girl who didn't charge by the half-hour, well, that was temporary. The truth was, he had become a La Rue family asset. The trust that his father was showing with this conversation was just another demonstration of his increasing stature and value.

Again, he smiled. He hoped his father had not noticed. He didn't think he had. Henri's head was down. He was stirring his coffee again. It seemed to be a nervous tic more than anything.

"Here's the thing," Henri said. "I need him to go away."

"Him?"

"Lemieux."

"Go away?" Guy said. He wasn't smiling anymore.

"What are you saying?" the son said.

"I'm saying, that priest needs to go away," the father said.

PART VI

27

The only time in nine days that Martin and Marie had left their room at the George V was on Day 6, when the front desk called and told them that the Presidential Suite had become available if they so desired. They did. But it was on the same floor, just the opposite end of the hallway. Their total time in said hallway was probably 45 seconds, maybe a minute.

The maids moved their clothing, which had grown in bulk as Marie had insisted on a fitting from Chanel on Day 4. Martin was fine with the same two suits, but he did agree to order additional underwear, socks and shirts from the men's haberdasher in the lobby.

They had been through the room service menu twice by Day 5, at which point the hotel agreed to allow meals to be delivered for lunch and dinner from Maxim's. Duck à l'orange for two was their lunch on that day, the ninth day. And if it was fabulous, well, nothing really tasted great anymore. And if the suite was breathtaking — two bedrooms, three bathrooms, a sitting room, a dining room, a study, and two televisions — it still seemed like jail, especially to Martin.

He wanted to go for a walk, anywhere, nowhere, just once around the block. She pleaded for him to stay inside. He insisted. He got dressed to go out. She physically barred the door. He put his arms on her shoulders and began to move her out of the way, physically, a little bit violently, and then he stopped himself. He had never hit Marie and he told himself that he never would. He would hide money from her, and cheat on her, but he wouldn't hit her. He had promised himself, and it was the only vow he had kept.

After a minute, Martin sat down again and picked at the chocolate mousse.

28

Clarice's other boyfriend was one of her former professors at the Sorbonne. Louis lived in the country with a wife and a daughter who was Clarice's age. He was funny and smart and, well, well endowed. And if Clarice brought the initiative to their sex, Louis indeed brought his own talents. "Big Lou" is what she sometimes whispered during sex, rhythmically, and he seemed to like it.

It had been Louis's tip about the devaluation of the franc that had enabled Clarice to convince Gerard that she could be a big asset to the family. He was a friend of a deputy to the finance minister, and he had told her while they cuddled after sex. It was just gossip, him showing off to her about who he knew and what he knew. Clarice never told him that she took advantage of his insider information, though. To Louis, she was young and sexy but not shady. He knew she was a successful broker now, but not one who colored outside the lines — and he had no idea that Clarice La Rue was one of *those* La Rues.

That night, after only the one time — "Big Lou is all tuckered out, baby" — Louis asked her, "So, what's new in the brokerage business?"

It was a nothing question, no more meaningful than if he had asked her about the weather, but it was the opening Clarice had been hoping for. She had already strategized a way to bring up the subject, but her preparations were unnecessary.

"The business, it's fine — buy, sell, collect the commissions, you know," she said.

Pause.

"But there was something interesting I heard yesterday at The Parquet," she said. Louis knew that The Parquet was the bar down the street from the bourse where the brokers unwound at the end of the trading day.

"Heard? What?"

"About this stock," Clarice said. And then she gave him the 30-second version of the story of The Riom Mining Company — sleepy company, steady dividend, all that.

"Really a colossal bore," she said. "The rumors don't make any sense to me."

At that point, Louis had raised himself from the pillow and was turned toward her in bed, leaning on his elbow. Intrigued. Yes.

"Have you bought any?" he asked.

"Not yet. Thinking about it. Want to know more. Want to understand the play. Don't want to be the one who gets played, you know."

Louis half shrugged, then sat up all the way.

"Riom Industries?"

"No, The Riom Mining Company."

"The Riom Mining Company," he said, and then he repeated it, more to himself than out loud.

After a few seconds, he said, "Don't wait too long. You know, I have friends, and that's what they all say."

The next day, the price of the stock jumped by two points.

There were three different big orders, two for 50,000 shares and one for 100,000. Clarice wondered which piece belonged to Big Lou.

At a price of 18, Clarice could cash out and record a profit of 38 percent. But she was not so inclined, not yet.

29

Sometimes, in addition to hitting him with the verbal abuse, Patrice would hit Lemieux with some physical abuse, too. She would squeeze his balls sometimes, which he really hated. This day, she brought out the little leather strap and worked over his ass while he fucked her. She thought she was hurting him, but she wasn't. Not much — and he very much enjoyed it. When they were done, he would stand in front of the full length mirror and look back over his shoulder, enjoying her handiwork. She never broke the skin, never raised a welt. All she left behind were red stripes that didn't really hurt when he sat down, not much, but felt warm to the touch for hours. Zebra-ass. That's what he always called it in his head.

Lemieux was having a drink in the bar afterward. He finished before Dr. Alain Benneville by a few minutes. When Benneville joined him at the table, he said, "Have you ever tried Nanette?"

"No."

"You should, my friend. Have you seen her?"

"No."

"Oh, your loss. She must be six feet tall, a goddamned Amazon. Blonde hair down to her ass. Legs to the sky. Oh, your loss."

"Maybe next time," Lemieux said, although he knew he was lying. He wasn't changing, mostly because he was afraid of changing.

The two of them, friends for years, talked about the weather and De Gaulle and whatnot, and then each of them ordered a second cognac. That's when Lemieux began to ask. It had been Benneville who had told him about the arsenic — how small doses over a period of months would make a person increasingly sick without killing them. With that knowledge, Lemieux had been able to spike Gerard's marmalade, which the old man spread on his breakfast bread every morning without fail. The priest made Gerard sick, and then got him to visit Lourdes, and then stopped the arsenic. Gerard got better quickly, and Lemieux got wealthy quickly.

Now, though, the priest was hoping to begin a new phase.

"What this time?" Benneville said.

"I don't want to make him sick."

"What, you want to kill him?"

"No, no — not sick and not dead. I just want him to be... confused."

"Christ, you're getting greedy — although Christ clearly has nothing to do with it," Benneville said.

They both went silent and sipped their drinks. Over the doctor's shoulder, Lemieux saw one of the girls walking by an open door at the end of the bar. She was wearing a pink robe that reached only to her thighs and Lemieux thought, well, Benneville was right. Nanette was a goddamned Amazon.

"Well," Benneville said.

"Tell me."

"I'm going to say it again: you are getting greedy. You're

already on the gravy train, and I don't know what else you might have to gain."

"Just tell me."

"All right," the doctor said. "Well, I guess, cyanide. That can cause confusion. I'm pretty sure, anyway, but it isn't something you come across every day in my profession. For one thing, I'd have to look up the dosage. I think this is trickier than the arsenic. An imbecile could have succeeded with the arsenic."

"Thanks," Lemieux said.

They sipped some more.

"He can't be dead," the priest said. "It doesn't work if he's dead. In fact, the whole thing collapses if he's dead."

"So, why take the risk?"

Lemieux didn't answer. He just sipped, and then waved to the bartender. One more for each of them.

They were quiet as they drank the last one. After five minutes, Benneville promised to work out the dosage. Lemieux reached into his jacket pocket and handed the doctor a white envelope. The priest had lied about how much money he was getting, lied lower, and the envelope contained five percent of the lower figure. It had been Lemieux's idea, and Benneville never refused.

"I guess I'm in the envelope culture now," he thought to himself after the two parted. On the walk back to the rectory, the priest could feel his trousers rubbing against the red stripes on his zebra-ass. He kind of liked the feeling.

30

For days, Sylvie replayed the meeting with the lawyer in her head. And every time she did it, she became even more depressed.

François Petit had met her in his spacious office. He didn't sit behind his desk, but on a chair next to a fireplace. Sylvie sat on the small sofa that faced him.

They had coffee and pleasantries for maybe five minutes. That was when she told Petit her real name — she had made the appointment as Mrs. Sylvie Gruen. And if the lawyer didn't choke on the coffee, he came close — after which, he placed the cup into the saucer and began what she laughingly came to refer to in her head as The Education of a Mob Wife.

"First of all, I appreciate the Mrs. Gruen subterfuge," Petit said. "You think you were protecting yourself, I'm sure, but you also were protecting me."

Sylvie looked confused.

"Mrs. La Rue, how many women in your current circumstance have gotten divorces?"

"Not many."

"Name one."

"Rosalie Parmentiere."

"And the grounds?"

"Well, her husband, he was, well..."

"Caught in the bathroom of the bus station with a human of the male persuasion," Petit said.

Sylvie looked shocked.

"A famous case, in your circle and in my circle, because it's the only case," he said. "That time, that one time, divorce was permitted. The wife was allowed to engage an attorney, and the papers were filed, and the results were uncontested, and the settlement was generous. One time. One in my memory."

Petit poured more coffee. Sylvie said nothing.

"We are not having this conversation, Mrs. La Rue. But you need to hear this before you leave. I will not represent you if you intend to go through with this divorce petition. There isn't an attorney of any repute who will do it. You might find someone, but he will end up regretting it and paying for it."

Petit paused, sipped.

"With a fractured skull, as likely as not," he said.

Sylvie knew that the path she was choosing was unconventional — but it was 1960, after all. Other parts of life were changing for women, why not this one?

Petit answered her question without her having to ask it.

"You are part of an old tradition," he said. "Is your husband hitting you?"

Sylvie shook her head.

"Even that isn't considered grounds for divorce in your world, as you well know. If he was hitting you, the best you could hope for would be an intervention by other members of your extended family. But that isn't this. Other than a bus station bathroom — this isn't that, right?"

Sylvie shook her head again.

"Just think about it this practically," Petit said. "You need more than your freedom from him, I assume. You need a financial settlement of some size in order to keep living what you consider to be a reasonable lifestyle. And, well, how are you going to get that? Even if you could engage an attorney, and even if you could get your petition approved, what exactly do you think you're going to be able to ask the court for in a settlement?"

"You wouldn't believe the money," she said.

"I would believe the money. But what can you prove? In all likelihood, all you can prove is what he tells the tax man. And if my guess is correct, what he tells the tax man isn't one-tenth of his true income. You sign the returns, right? One-tenth?"

Yes, she signed the returns. Henri's only listed income came from his salary at the uniform store.

"One-fiftieth," she said. "That's a guess, but—"

"And that's the problem in a nutshell. You can't get a lawyer, you probably can't win if you can get a lawyer, and even if you could get a lawyer and you did win, you wouldn't get enough in the settlement to rent more than a cold-water flat on the fourth floor of a shit building on the worst street in the 20th."

And that was that.

31

Roger Cornette was sitting in his office, poring over some of the endless paperwork, when Gerard walked in. Cornette was his oldest friend, a running buddy since primary school. And if time and circumstances created some distance — the circumstances being that one man was in charge of a mob family and the other was in charge of the Mazarine Library — time also held them together, time and a love of literature.

The magnificent reading room outside was nearly deserted — two old men, two massive texts on the tables in front of them, one with his good eye just inches from the page, the eyeglasses perched on his forehead. It was early, and students would arrive later in the day.

"Old-man hours," is what Cornette said he worked. He let himself into the library soon after seven and was done by three. He insisted that all of his meetings be in the morning, and all of his massaging of benefactors be at lunch, not dinner. It was 8:30 when Gerard arrived, a full 90 minutes before the library officially opened. But the guard knew who he was and let him in. Old-man hours.

"Enough with this shit," Gerard said. He tossed a copy of a Zane Grey onto the desk blotter in front of Cornette.

"And hello to you, too, old friend."

Gerard harrumphed.

"The American Westerns hold no appeal for you anymore, I see."

"We need a change," Gerard said. "I can't deal with it. No more cattle rustlers. No more stoic sheriffs. We need something new. Now."

For years they had been in a book club that contained exactly two members. They would choose a genre — Russians in the 19th century, Americans in the early 20th century, lately American Westerns — and read their way through a selected canon. The two of them would choose the genre, and then Cornette would choose the individual books, and then they would discuss each one upon completion. Except that Gerard seemed to hate everything after only a little while, and the Westerns were no exception.

Their book club was less about the books than the club, and they both knew it. It was such an odd relationship — mobster, librarian, crazy — but it had endured over the decades because they worked at it, and because they avoided talking about Gerard's typical workday, and because they could use the books as the mortar that held the foundation in place.

Cornette steered the discussion to a new genre — "Maybe the Spaniards? We haven't gone near them, I don't think" — when the guard appeared in the office doorway.

"Delivery," he said.

"They're early."

The guard shrugged, and Cornette stood up with the customary old-man sound effects.

"I have to sign for this," he said, leaving Gerard alone in the office. After a few seconds, his mind wandered back to the where it had been wandering a lot more often lately.

They were sitting on a bench across from Sacré Coeur. Early 1917, he figured. The scaffolding still covered the building, just as it had for most of Gerard's life.

"They say it's going to be beautiful, breathtaking," he said. "I mean, I guess."

"Oh, you can see the beauty beneath," Celeste said.

"I guess."

"Of course, you can see it."

"How do you know what I can see?"

"Because I've looked into your eyes," Celeste said.

They'd had sex just the one time, just the night before — both of them drunk, fumbling around in the back seat of Gerard's car. It was his first time, but he told her it wasn't. It was her first time, she said, and he believed her.

He put his arm around her on the bench, and they stared at Sacré Coeur and at the sunset. They didn't talk much. Theirs was the definition of young love, the sweetest love, the most uncomplicated love.

When it was time for her to go, she reached into her bag and handed Gerard a book, The Count of Monte Cristo. She said, "I think you'll like it."

"Not much of a reader," he said.

"Just try. Like I said, I think you'll like it."

He really wasn't much of a reader, but he would do anything for Celeste at that point. He cracked the book open as soon as he got back to his apartment and found himself drawn in almost immediately. He finished it in three days and nights, staying up until 3 a.m. twice.

The next Saturday, in the back seat again, with her breasts illuminated by the moonlight, they talked about the book. Gerard was torn by the theme of revenge that dominated the story, and would be for the rest of his life. There were times when he would be as primally vengeful as Dantes, the main character. At other times, he would be repelled by the very notion of living your life that way.

That night, in the back seat, that's what they talked about. And in the end, Celeste said, "I told you that you could see beneath the scaffolding."

"So, the Spaniards?" Roger Cornette said. Back from the delivery, he was carrying two books, two copies of Don Quixote.

"Kind of a cliché to start there, no?"

"You have a better choice?"

"Not really."

"So, just being disagreeable on principle?"

"As ever," Gerard said.

PART VII

32

For the last four days, Henri had directed Freddy to send one of his guys to sit in the lobby of the George V. His only direction to Freddy was, "It has to be someone Michel has never met."

"No problem there. He's never come to our place. I don't think he's ever picked up a delivery at Gare du Nord or shipped any product out that way. I've probably got four guys he's never laid eyes on."

"Good," Henri said. "Maybe rotate a couple of guys through."

"And what do they do?"

"Just fucking sit there. Wear a decent suit. Sit there, say nine to five. Drink coffee. Read the papers. Have a nice lunch on you. No alcohol until after four. Tell each guy to look for guys hanging out who kind of look like he does."

"Young gorillas, then," Freddy said.

"You said it, not me, but yes. If they see something, call. Otherwise, check in around lunchtime and again at five."

Henri had promised himself he wouldn't get involved, that he would let Michel handle it. But the whole thing had never made sense to him. It just never added up, never sat right. Why would Michel volunteer? And why had he been Martin's butt buddy for the last few months after a couple of years when they had no visible relationship at all? It just didn't make sense. And, after a week, Henri couldn't help himself. This seemed minimal to him, a light surveillance, nothing more. What was the harm? The only cost was the lunch bill and drinks between four and five, which were really between two and five — but who could blame Freddy's kids? It was a beautiful lobby, and it was a handsome bar, and it was shit duty.

33

And on Day 11 the job went to Pascal, a particularly brutish specimen who, in Henri's memory, always looked as if he was going to bust the top button on his shirt. Henri thought about it enough that he sometimes shielded his eyes with his hand when he was close to Pascal. He didn't know the kid's name but he knew the button. The fucking button could blind him.

The kid had been sitting in the lobby, bored, since just after nine. Coffee. Piss. Newspaper. Another coffee. Another piss. Another paper, *L'Equipe*. He was reading about some hurdler preparing for the Rome Olympics when he saw three guys walk in. Two took a seat on one side of the lobby, the other on the other side. That was the first thing that struck Pascal, that the three of them didn't sit together.

For the first time in three hours, he felt awake. All three of the guys who looked like him ordered coffee and looked around, mostly over at the elevators. And the thing was, they did look like him. He hadn't been sure what Freddy meant when he said it, but he understood now. Young. Burly. Well dressed. A little out of place, if you were paying attention. Like him.

Pascal walked across to the bank of pay phones near the front desk and made a call to the uniform store. Henri La Rue wasn't there, which was fine with Pascal — because Henri La Rue made him nervous. So he left the message. It seemed stupid, but those were the instructions he was given.

The message: "Three guys who look like me, sitting in the lobby, staring at the elevators."

34

Michel: "So, you've got it?"

Ronny: "Couldn't be fucking simpler."

Michel: "One more time."

Ronny: "I'm not an imbecile."

Michel: "I'm not saying you're an imbecile."

Ronny: "Then why?"

Michel: "I am paying you up front, after all."

Ronny: "But, for fuck's sake."

Michel: "Just one more time. Humor me."

Ronny: "Taxi to the George V."

Michel: "And?"

Ronny: "I tell the cabbie to wait."

Michel: "Right. Right."

Ronny: "Courtesy phones by the front desk."

Michel: "And you ask for..."

Ronny: "Martin La Rue."

Michel: "And you tell him..."

Ronny: "That my name is Ronny..."

Michel: "And that you're..."

Ronny: "One of Michel's guys..."

Michel: "And that..."

Ronny: "Michel says it's all taken care of."

Michel: "And?"

Ronny: "That Michel will meet you in the lobby."

Michel: "When?"

Ronny: "In 20 minutes."

Michel: "Good, good, 20 minutes. And then?"

Ronny: "Back in the taxi, straight to Montparnasse Station, on the 6 p.m. back to Marseille."

35

Henri was just walking back from Gartner's, where he ate by himself and had the egg on the Salad Niçoise, goddammit, when one of the drivers from the uniform store ran into him on the sidewalk.

"Hurry," he said.

"Why?"

"They didn't tell me. Just hurry."

When he got to the store, Passy gave him the message.

"Fuck, fuck, fuck," Henri said.

"Boss, what?" Passy said.

"Fuck." Long pause. "Fuck."

Henri's driver, Donnie, was sitting where usually sat — in the far corner, chatting with the seamstress he had been fucking for the last six months. Sylvie. "Be careful, Sylvies are tough — I know."

"Just pussy, boss."

"So you say."

Henri knew where to look, saw him, and yelled, "DONNIE," and both Donnie and Sylvie nearly fell off their chairs.

"CAR. NOW."

Donnie ran past him. It would take less than two minutes for him to pull the car around front. It was during those two minutes that the phone rang again. Passy answered, listened, and handed the receiver to Henri.

"Mr. La Rue," is how Pascal began, but he was having trouble with the Rue part, elongating the R part before he got to the UE part. It seemed like it took five seconds.

"Take a breath and fucking spit it out," Henri said.

"I might be imagining this, because I'm pretty fucking paranoid at this point," Pascal said. "But a guy just came into the hotel and walked over to the courtesy phones — you know, the ones by the front desk, the ones where you can call up to a room."

"Courtesy phone. I've got it."

"Well, the guy, he made a call. It was quick — like, maybe five seconds. Maybe less than five seconds. And when he hung up, well, he looked over at the one jamoke sitting by himself across the lobby, one of the guys who's been drinking coffee and staring at the elevators, and he tipped his hat."

"The courtesy phone guy, he tipped his hat."

"Yes, sir."

Henri handed the receiver the Passy and sprinted out the door of the uniform store. He stood on the sidewalk for about 15 seconds before the car roared to a stop in front of him. He spent the whole 15 seconds muttering, "Fuck, fuck, fuck."

36

artin hung up the phone, and Marie looked at him.

"One of Michel's guys. Ronny."

"And?"

"He says Michel has something for me in the lobby. Says it looks like it's all over. Twenty minutes, he'll be there."

"Looks like? I don't know. Who is this Ronny?"

"One of Michel's guys."

At which point, which Martin put on a freshly pressed suit — the maids took the clothes every morning and had them back before lunch. While he was dressing, he and Marie argued. That was fine, but she wasn't stopping him this time. He was back in control. He had Michel's balls in his pocket, and Michel had taken care of a problem that really wasn't his fault in the first place. It was just bad luck. It could have happened to anyone.

"Have you ever met this Ronny?" Marie said.

"No, but so what?"

"I don't know, it's just—"

"Look, nobody knows we're here except Gerard, Henri, and Michel."

"And this Ronny."

"He's Michel's guy," Martin said. "Stop worrying."

He looked at his watch. Twenty minutes on the dot. He decided to tie his necktie extra slowly, to tie his shoes deliberately, to go for a piss that he didn't really need. Twenty minutes would be a half-hour. He was in charge, after all, not Michel.

He checked himself in the mirror one final time, and Marie said, "Are you sure about this? Does he know how dangerous this is?"

"It's all covered, baby."

"It just seems so, I don't know—"

"You're just stir crazy."

"Maybe," Marie said. "Maybe you're right. You're probably right. But part of me, I don't know—"

Martin grabbed her two hands with his two hands. And while he looked into her eyes, Martin said, "No worries — I own him, baby."

He almost skipped out the door.

37

The drive from the uniform store to the George V wasn't three miles, but Paris traffic was Paris traffic, and it might have taken a half-hour if Donnie followed all of the rules. Now, in normal circumstances, Donnie saw the rules more as guidelines — and on this day, in this crisis, the guidelines became, well, blurrier. He actually drove on the sidewalk at one point, just for a few hundred feet, and completely blew through a red light at Rue de Monceau, leaning on his horn and likely causing an accident behind him. But it was behind him, and Henri never looked back.

Fucking Martin. If he said it once during that car ride — 18 minutes, he thought, when he checked his watch just before arriving at the hotel — he said it 10 times. Fucking Martin. He said it almost as a reflex. He'd been saying it since he was about 16, after all, since his younger brother became old enough to get into trouble and since it became Henri's fraternal responsibility to bail him out. This was just one in a line, a long line — although the problems were almost never potentially lethal, like this one. Financial, reputational, sexual — those were Martin's typical screw-ups. Lethal, not so much. So, this was different but it was the same. Fucking Martin.

The adrenaline built as Donnie careened through the afternoon traffic. Henri was preparing to act, not necessarily to think. A million notions did fly through his head, but focusing was not something of which he was capable, not then. But the ideas did fly, almost in rotation, and one was more prominent than the rest. That was: Michel. Where was he, and what might his involvement be?

There was a chance that the soldiers in the lobby belonged to Michel, were employed by Michel, and were there as protection for Martin. There was a chance, yes. That only made sense, though, if Michel sensed that the remnants of Jean Garreau's little gang were preparing to act. But if that was the case, why would he take them on in the lobby? Why not on the street? And who was the guy on the telephone who tipped his hat to the soldiers?

All of that played in a loop through Henri's head as Donnie wove in and out of traffic, coming within inches of a dozen neighboring fenders and, at least once, clipping off the side view mirror of a parked car. He was driving so rambunctiously that the vehicles with whom he was sharing the streets responded in the time-honored Paris tradition, by leaning on their horns. There was a cacophony as they drove. It was almost constant. But Henri almost didn't hear it, so consumed was he with that loop running through his head.

All he knew — and it was his very first instinct, as soon as he received the phone message — was that the gorillas in the lobby were not likely friendly to Martin, and that the phone call and the tip of the cap surely seemed like a signal of sorts being relayed to the unfriendly gorillas, and that he needed to be there. He had promised himself, promised that he wasn't going to get involved, that he was going to let Michel handle it, but the phone messages had changed everything. Good intentions or not, what was he supposed to do? Fucking Martin.

The car screeched to a halt right in front of the George V, nearly knocking over one of the doormen who had come to the curb to open the door. Henri rushed past him, almost knocking him down a second time, and into the lobby.

He scanned the room quickly, eyes darting. Within about three seconds, he spotted Freddy's guy. Even from 50 feet away he noticed how nervous the kid was, fumbling with his hands in front of him as he sat. He looked around and then he saw the other guys, the unknown soldiers — two on one side of the lobby, one on the other. They didn't see him because, as Freddy's guy had said, they were glancing — casually but persistently — in the direction of the elevators.

Freddy's guy, the other guys. Another quick scan and Henri saw the bank of courtesy phones near the front desk, six phones in all, a privacy divider separating them. None of the phones were being used. One couple was checking in at the front desk.

It all seemed normal enough, a luxury hotel in the late afternoon, nothing more, nothing less. Henri decided to head toward the elevators. He buttoned his jacket after feeling reflexively for his shoulder holster. He didn't did run, didn't rush, but he did stride with purpose.

38

Normally, Martin was the kind of guy who mashed the elevator button every 3.2 seconds until it showed up, the kind who began cursing after maybe 10 seconds (or three mashes). That day was different, though. That day, Martin luxuriated in the silence of the hallway, the long, open hallway. No mashes, no curses — even as 10 seconds grew to about 30.

It was over, finally. And if it was long-past due, days past due, well, that was a conversation with Michel that Martin was anticipating with some excitement. The whole thing was perfect, really. Michel was taking care of the problem — a problem that wasn't even Martin's fault. He was taking care of it because Martin owned him and would continue to own him. And it was all happening just slowly enough that Martin could still berate Michel, still emphasize Michel's current vulnerabilities.

Martin stood there in the hallway, hands in pockets. He felt the house keys in his left pocket and thought for a second and laughed. Because Michel's balls were still his, still in his pocket, and there was nothing his cousin could do about it. That night in Lourdes would remain the gift that kept on giving for the foreseeable future — certainly for as long as Gerard was alive. When Martin caught Michel in the midst of cheating the family in that side deal, the entire dynamic changed.

Because, while every La Rue was a pragmatist when it came to money — and Michel brought in the cash from his heroin operation, without question — Gerard and Henri, and Gerard especially, would not tolerate the betrayal. At the minimum, they would bust Michel down to being an employee, not a partner — and millions of francs stood in that balance. And when he thought about that, Martin just smiled some more. Because, on the one hand, Michel was paying him, and kissing his ass, and cleaning up whatever needed cleaning up in the short term and the medium term. And, on the other hand, Martin would make sure that Michel's betrayal was known to Gerard and Henri in the long term — which meant that Martin would get his cut of the income Michel would ultimately be forced to forfeit, the millions of francs that currently stood in the balance. Win-win — and who was the idiot now?

Finally, the elevator arrived. It was empty. Two floors lower, the doors opened and a woman pushing a pram got in. Martin hated children — Marie was barren, thank God — and especially babies. But that day, he leaned over and smiled at the little girl and cooed. In reply, she laughed and farted like a longshoreman.

He laughed. The mom laughed. She shrugged and said, "We just started her on applesauce."

What a glorious day. The elevator door opened again, and this time a man and woman entered. There was just enough room for them and Martin and the mom and the longshoreman. A mishmash of "pardon me"/"no worries" followed, and then everyone stared at the numbers above the door, as one does.

Martin couldn't help smiling as the elevator door opened. The sun was shining outside — outside! — and the whole stupid thing had been resolved without any real damage to him. Pressed into the back corner of the elevator as the rest maneuvered their way out, longshoreman first, he felt the keys in his pocket again. He felt Michel's balls again. They were his, still.

39

In just a few seconds, Henri had strode past the front desk, past the courtesy phones, and into the sitting area of the lobby, the place where couches lined the walls and clusters of chairs surrounded dainty tables — some with two chairs, some with four.

Freddy's guy was at one of the twos, by himself. He started to stand when he saw Henri approach the area, but Henri got him to sit back down with a hard stare. He was pretty sure no one had noticed the interaction.

The Garreau soldiers were closer to the elevators, flanking it on either side — the pair sitting to the left of the elevators, the single sitting to the right. There was an empty table, also on the right but well behind the soldiers and the elevators. That was where Henri sat. He hoped that the service was as customarily shitty as it was at most snooty places like the George V. The last thing he needed was a little old man in a black coat trying to take his drink order.

From his seat, he could see that Freddy's guy was starting at him while, at the same time, the other gorillas were staring at the elevators and sitting up just a little straighter every time they heard the muffled ding of an arriving car. Henri looked at Freddy's guy and nonchalantly patted his shoulder holster. Freddy's guy replied by mimicking the gesture. Good.

Henri looked again at the elevators. Nothing yet. There was a knot of three people waiting, and one guy was beating on the button. They must have been slow.

Henri sized up the geometry and hoped that Freddy's guy had done the same. He would have a clear shot at the two on the left, and Freddy's guy would have a clear shot at the one on the right. With his open hands, he made an X, left to right, and then chopped the left hand over the right. Freddy's guy nodded, acting like he got it, but Henri couldn't be sure. The kid looked petrified.

The bell of an arriving elevator dinged, and now there were five people sitting up just a little bit straighter. But the only person who emerged from the elevator was a thousand-year-old woman wearing an enormous pink hat. Just lugging that thing around must have exhausted her. Anyway, she creeped out, and the three people waiting got in, and the elevator entry area was empty again.

From his seat, Henri couldn't tell if there was one of those clock-things on the top, a half-dial with a moving hand that told you what floor the elevator was on. There must have been one, he figured — and the two gorillas on the left must have been able to see it. He would have to be guided by their reactions. If they began to tense up, to sit up straighter, maybe to get their shooting hand in position, then he would do the same.

Ten seconds.

Fifteen seconds.

Then he sensed what the two soldiers were seeing. One casually unbuttoned the jacket button that he had unbuttoned and re-buttoned at least twice in the minute or so that Henri had been sitting there. The other sat up just a bit straighter, but what

Henri noticed mostly was how his face tensed up. Henri could only see the kid in profile, but the look was obvious — the look, and also the subtle movement of his lips. The kid was talking to himself, steeling himself for what was to come.

The soft ding, muffled so as not to be annoying to the patrons in the lobby, was deafening to Henri's hyper-focused ears.

The doors opened.

Nothing.

One second.

Two seconds.

Finally, something: a blue pram nosing its way out of the door, a blue pram pushed by a pretty blonde in a matching blue dress.

One second.

Next came a middle-aged couple, the woman first, then the man. She was a half-step ahead of him and, once clear of the elevator, she instinctively slowed to walk beside the man. Probably married.

One second.

Two seconds.

Then came Martin.

When he thought about it later — when he was telling the story to Sylvie that night, because she was the only one he told — the whole thing seemed to happen in slow motion.

Henri saw Martin. Big, goofy smile on his face. He would never forget that for some reason. Big, goofy smile.

Next, he looked at the soldiers who were there to kill Martin. They, too, were looking at the elevator. They saw Martin, but there was the slightest hesitation while the three of them all made eye contact, as if confirming with each other that Martin was, indeed, Martin.

The slightest hesitation.

One second, no more.

Then, the three of them rose at once. The guy sitting by himself was clumsy enough that he knocked over the spindly little table next to his chair. They rose, the three of them, and they reached for their guns. Henri saw that. He saw at least two pistols.

And then Henri fired.

X with the hands. Chop, chop, left over right.

Henri fired three times, actually. He hit the first kid sitting on the left cleanly, right in the back of the head. He winged the second kid, who staggered a step and grabbed on to one of those potted palms that littered all swanky hotel lobbies. The tree helped him keep his feet, but it also made Henri's second shot easier. Right in the face, easier.

And then, as he remembered it, Henri felt as if he heard about five more shots. He had no idea how many the guy on the right, the soldier sitting on his own, managed to get off. He only knew for sure that the guy ended up dead, very dead — and that Freddy's guy ended up with a smoking pistol in his hand and a look on his face like somebody who, well, who had killed a guy for the first time.

All around them was a screaming pandemonium. There were probably 30 people in the lobby — guests and employees — and they were all yelling and hiding under tables and behind curtains and wherever. The employees were all behind the front desk, only the tops of their heads visible.

Henri walked the 20 steps over to Freddy's guy.

"Great job, great job — now, right to the car," Henri said. He pointed out to where Donnie was standing with the car door opened.

Then Henri turned and looked at Martin. He was on his knees, peeking out from behind a gold-plated standing ashtray that sat beneath the elevator buttons.

"Well, are you fucking coming or not?" Henri said. He turned and walked out of the lobby, out to the car, and Martin ran past him before he got there.

The three of them crowded into the back seat. The car pulled away from the curb, and Donnie began with his maneuvers, and Henri said, "Don't, Donnie. Just get lost in the traffic." After a minute or so, he could hear the police sirens in the distance.

As the adrenaline ebbed, Martin was still shaking. Henri noticed but said nothing. He purposely ignored his brother. Instead, he leaned over him — Martin was in the middle — and asked Freddy's guy, "What's your name, kid?"

"Pascal," he said.

"My best man, my oldest friend, is Pascal. Passy. Do you know him? Have you ever met?"

"Heard the name, never met."

"Well, he's Passy," Henri said. "And from now on, you're Little Passy."

With that, he could see the smile on the kid's face as he sat back in the seat. Henri was pretty sure he smiled, too. Martin just sat there, shaking. During the whole car ride, the older brother never said a word to the younger brother — not a word of comfort, not a word of admonishment. Not a word.

PART VIII

40

Henri practiced the whole dance for a day, practiced it every which way, and ultimately decided that two meetings would be better than one. The first would be with Martin alone.

He chose a neutral site — The Magnolia, a café on Rue des Abbesses. At 10:30, the breakfast business was over and the lunch business was more than an hour away. Most of the waiters were pressed into light cleaning duty — dusting this, wiping that — before the lunch rush. Henri arrived early and chose a table in the back corner. He was the only customer.

The only other person who knew what was happening was Sylvie. They had had a huge argument a couple of days before, a fight about what he was spending on Polly. She waved around some Chanel invoice that she had found in a suit of his that she was sending to the cleaners, and screamed about "your fucking whores," and went on and on — all through dinner and until lights out. Henri slept in the guest bedroom and then admitted defeat — or, rather, celebrated victory — by doubling Sylvie's monthly allowance and adding 50 percent to her household budget. He considered it a bargain.

So, only Sylvie knew, not Gerard, not anyone else. The story in *France-Soir* had been gory on the one hand but splendidly vague on the other. The dead men were identified as small-time hoods reportedly associated with the Garreau crime family. The person who killed them was unknown. The reason also was unknown. Bystanders guessed that the target was someone coming out of the elevator, but no one had a better description than "middle-aged man in a suit." In other words, like every other person staying at the George V. As for the hotel employees, they knew nothing — not about the shooter, not about the man in the elevator, not about whether or not the sky was blue. God bless the George V, and the rules of old money. Actually, it was really only one rule: I saw nothing.

As far as Gerard was concerned, the hero of the day had been Little Passy. Henri got credit for ordering the rotation of Freddy's soldiers through the George V lobby, and Michel got a demerit because he hadn't thought of the same thing, but as far as Gerard's mental score-keeping went, that was it. Little Passy practiced the story and never deviated. He told Freddy, and Freddy told Henri, and Henri told Gerard. It was an easy lie because it was mostly the truth: the three gorillas in the lobby, the guy at the courtesy phone who signaled them, Martin coming out of the elevator, bang, bang, bang. All Little Passy had to leave out was the call to Henri and Henri's arrival on the scene.

"Best that way," Sylvie said.

"I guess, but why?" Henri said.

"Neater, cleaner," she said. "Make the kid the hero."

"The kid is a hero. At that age, I couldn't have done it. I would have wet myself. Christ, I nearly wet myself anyway."

"It's a nice story," Sylvie said. "Young hero. Nice story, all wrapped up in a bow. In his old age, I think Gerard probably likes nice stories."

"I don't know, he's a cynical old fuck."

"But he was very sick and then he got better," Sylvie said. "I think old Uncle Gerard might be looking on the bright side more than he did. He'll like this, this Little Passy fable. And I guess, well, I don't know what the briefcase priest will think, but he might just like a nice story, too. And the farther away those two stay from this whole thing, the better for you."

On that point, Henri was in full agreement. He needed to be able to massage this situation, turn it into the opportunity that it was. He had gone through it all several times, and his mind couldn't stop. It was still going when Martin walked into The Magnolia, although walked didn't quite cut it. His younger brother shuffled more than he walked, and he was slightly slumped over, and his suit was wrinkled, and he hadn't shaved.

"Back home now, right?" Henri said.

Martin nodded.

"Marie, she's okay?"

Another nod.

They ordered something to eat, and Martin barely picked at his eggs. Henri, on the other hand, was ravenous. He just shoveled the food into his mouth, and Martin watched him in silence.

"Nothing to say?" Henri said.

Martin shrugged.

"We've been through worse," Henri said.

"I nearly fucking died."

"But you didn't. Like I said, we've been through worse."

Martin said nothing. He shrugged again, and then he closed his eyes. Henri thought he was oddly distant. He thought Martin was going to cry.

"All right," Henri said.

With that, the going-to-cry look changed into something more immediate, more present, more fearful.

"Don't worry," Henri said. "There won't be any recriminations, and I don't want anything."

He wiped a wedge of his toast in the yolk on his plate.

"Well, I do want one thing."

Pause.

"I demand one thing."

Martin's eyes widened when he heard the word "demand." Henri saw that and then he went back to wiping his plate with the last piece of toast.

"What I demand is the truth about you and Michel," Henri said. And then, in the space of about two seconds, Martin's eyes went wide with alarm and then soft with resignation.

And then Martin started talking. He told Henri about the night in Lourdes when Michel nearly died in the midst of an illicit heroin deal — all heroin deals were illicit but this was worse because it was a secret being kept from La Rue Family Inc. He told Henri how he had saved Michel's life and killed four men in the process, and how he was now taking half of Michel's quarterly payment in exchange for keeping the betrayal from Henri and Gerard.

Martin talked for two or three minutes straight, and when he was done, he exhaled and slumped back in his seat.

"Feels good to get it out, doesn't it?"

"I'm not sure about that."

"Trust me: better out than in," Henri said. "You know, like Mama used to say when one of us was sick and she was poking around in the bathroom closet, looking for the enema bag."

At that, Martin laughed for the first time in two days, and then Henri sent him on his way. He had some thinking to do now that Martin had told him the secret. The next meeting, a dinner the following night, would include the three of them.

41

Thursdays after lunch, Father Lemieux left Gerard's house on the top of the butte and headed to the office for his weekly catch-up meeting with the staff that did all of the real financial work for the archdiocese. Lemieux did make some of the big decisions but he mostly just signed off on the dozens of smaller decisions made by the staff. Then, the next morning, he sat with the cardinal and walked him through the numbers.

Most days, Lemieux walked down from the apartment behind Sacré Coeur to the chancery. He tended to get a ride in the other direction, but from the top of Montmartre down to the archdiocese office near Notre Dame was an easy stretch of the legs. Guy checked on a map and made his best estimate: a little less than three miles. But it walked much faster because it was so downhill, especially at the beginning. He figured it would take less than an hour.

Guy sat on a bench outside of Sacré Coeur and hid behind a copy of *France-Soir*. The second-day coverage about the big shootout at the George V was all over the front page, and Guy gobbled up the story like someone with VD reading a story about penicillin. Still no leads about the shooter, still nothing on the identity of the intended victim, just a lot of hand-wringing by political types about the lawlessness of the Paris gang culture.

To which, Guy thought, "Nobody got hurt. Well, no civilians. Move on."

He had a dozen questions about what happened, but it wasn't his place to ask. Not yet. He knew that his Uncle Martin had been hiding out, and that Guy himself had been sleeping on Nico's couch for a few nights, here and there, just to keep his mother happy. He figured that Martin had been the target, and that some combination of La Rue guns had been employed, but that was it. He knew not to ask, to wait to be told. He also knew that he was looking forward to a night in his own bed.

Fucking Nico. The age difference, only four years; well, Guy couldn't believe how much more energy Nico had. Work every afternoon and night — and he really was good at the work, diligent and organized — and then play every night with Guy as his running buddy/chaperone. It really was killing him. The all-timer had happened earlier that week, when Guy actually fell asleep on Nico's couch while one of the girls they had brought back to the apartment was blowing him. He couldn't believe how insulted she was when he began snoring. It was only for a second or two, but he heard himself, and then he heard her screaming loud enough for Nico to come out of the bedroom, bellowing over and over, "You know, I'm good at this, you fucking asshole."

Guy juggled the schedule after that and gave himself consecutive days off for the first time in forever, Wednesday and Thursday. He slept 16 hours on Wednesday and was looking forward to the Thursday walk down the butte. From behind the newspaper, he saw Lemieux leave Gerard's house. He checked his watch: 1 p.m.

Down the steps, then more steps, then more — they easily

gave up a couple of hundred feet of elevation in the first quarter-mile. After that, it was flatter but still slightly downhill — down Boulevard de Magenta for a long stretch, and then a right turn onto Boulevard de Strasbourg for another long stretch. Women were out doing their shopping, and old men were playing boules, and the kids were enjoying recess in the schoolyard when they passed two different schools. Guy was about 200 feet behind Lemieux, and the distance could have been greater seeing as how Guy thought he knew where the priest was headed.

He walked, and he kept an eye on Lemieux, and he daydreamed. Some of it was about his place in the family business, and how much it had improved in the previous few months. Some of it was about his relationship with his father, and how that had improved, too. For years — since he was about 12 — his father rarely avoided an opportunity to let Guy know what a disappointment he was, what a fuck-up he was. But lately, well, they had grown so much closer and his father had shown so much more trust in him. And how that was great on the one hand. And how it was fucked-up on the other hand. Henri La Rue didn't love Guy for himself but only for his ability to be a competent, money-making member of La Rue Family Inc.

Guy thought about all of that, but he also thought about that lunch with his father and the talk about Lemieux. He didn't exactly say the words, but did he want his son to kill the priest? Is that what he was now to his father, a capable hit man? And when he thought about it, and if he was being honest with himself, well, he didn't hate the notion. And the fact that he didn't hate it, well, why didn't it bother him more than it did? Why didn't he hate it?

They made a couple of more turns, and then Lemieux climbed the steps and entered the chancery. From what the priest had said before in Guy's presence, the priest met with his financial staff from 3-5 p.m. The meeting with the cardinal was Friday morning at 8 a.m. He would be back in Montmartre for lunch.

But what about in between? Guy walked down the block and across the street to a café and sat outside under an umbrella. He had a clear view of the chancery steps from his seat. One coffee, then one red wine, then another.

42

Stockbrokers drank at The Parquet after work. Newspaper reporters drank at a placed called The Inkwell. They really weren't that different, the two places, not physically and not in their clientele. Both were full of men — almost entirely full of men — who spent their days shouting and using the word "fuck" a lot, in all of its declensions.

The Inkwell was where Clarice picked up Robby Laperriere, the financial columnist at *Le Monde*. She knew, from asking one of the bartenders, that the financial reporters were the earliest customers because they had the earliest deadlines. They had to be written about 4 p.m. and were drinking by 4:15. Most of the citywide reporters worked until six and arrived soon after. The sportswriters worked later, depending on the event they were covering. Some showed up after 11. The poor saps working night cops wouldn't be in until after midnight.

Anyway, Laperriere was on his customary stool at 4:22. Clarice was on the stool next to him at 4:34. The two of them were in a cab to Laperriere's apartment at 6:10. They were naked, finished, and talking about a restaurant at seven on the nose.

Which was when he said, "You know, you're too young and too pretty for it to have been that easy."

"You doubt your charms?"

"I own a mirror. So... what the hell?"

At which point, she told him. She had a request, and it wasn't a restaurant. She wanted him to mention The Riom Mining Company in his next column. Something in the last section of the column, the dot-dot-dot section of rumors and one-liners. Something on the order of, "Lots of chatter about the sleepy Riom Mining Company. Normally, the stock is better than valerian for insomniacs. But something is going on."

"Really, is that all?" Laperriere said.

"It's not even unethical."

"Blowjob-for-a-column? I think that might be unethical."

"But that's not what it is."

"She says, as she wipes her mouth."

"You hurt my feelings."

"You're pretty transparent."

"And you're pretty much a dick."

"Which was just in the mouth you've been wiping."

"You talk to all your girls like this?"

"Only the ones blowing me for column inches."

"Your most impressive inches, by far."

"And now who's hurting whose feelings? Anyway, tell me again how it isn't unethical."

"It's because you'll just be reporting facts that are available to anybody — on the bourse or off the bourse. Because anybody who happens to be paying attention knows that what I'm telling you is true."

"What facts?"

"That there has been unusual activity in the stock, unusually high volumes. It's up over three points in the last three days."

They talked about it a little more while they got dressed, and then Clarice left, unfed. As it turned out, Laperriere went back to the office and rewrote the dot-dot-dot section of his column. The item turned out to be pretty much word for word what she had pitched to him, even the valerian bit — with a few other numbers thrown in just to demonstrate that he had done a little bit of reporting.

The next day, the stock was up two more points. That was five points in a week. The price was now up to 23, and her gain was now 77 percent — well north of the 50 percent she needed to fulfill her quarterly goal for the La Rue family investors.

And while she was tempted to pull the trigger on the trade, she waited.

43

The restaurant Henri chose for dinner was the quite fabulous La Tour d'Argent. It was way too nice, not a La Rue business meeting kind of place at all. The last time Henri had been there was with Sylvie on an anniversary — two years earlier. Maybe three. He chose it because he wanted to project an aura of celebration — Martin was safe, and the problem was solved, and such like. Whether they would see through it or not really didn't matter — they would know the truth within five minutes of the appetizers being served. But, if it kept Michel even a hair off-balance walking in, that was good enough.

Martin's revelation from the morning before required a bit of a rethink, but just a bit. He and Sylvie ran through the possibilities over dinner, and while they weren't 100 percent sure about some of the details, they both agreed on the main foundational point: that Gerard could not be permitted to find out.

"That one's really non-negotiable," Sylvie said. "I mean, it doesn't work if the old man knows. It doesn't work in any way, shape or form."

Henri nodded, and then he smiled. Sylvie had always been

his most loyal lieutenant, even more than Passy. She had always been his chief strategist, his most reliable sounding board. It was old school — the wife being the silent power behind the power. It was the thing that caused the cleavage between mother and daughter, Clarice insisting that it was 1960, and that a woman belonged at the table.

But the reason he smiled was not because of the quality of Sylvie's advice — it was because of her engagement. She had been in that malaise for months, ever since Henri sabotaged her lover in that bourse scandal. And if Sylvie didn't know about Henri's involvement, it didn't matter. For months, it had been as if she had been living in a balloon made of cotton gauze, everything a bit hazy, never quite present.

But now, this business with Martin and Michel and the George V, it had seemingly lifted the clouds. Sylvie was focused again, smart again, cynical and funny and cutting again. Like when she said, "I'm not much for pornography, as you know, and certainly not *that* kind, but I'd pay good money to watch you fuck Martin and Michel at the same time."

At the restaurant, Henri arrived early, then Martin on time, then Michel five minutes late. A power move, being late. Maybe it was just a reflex, not a recognition of the current reality. Whatever, Henri thought.

They ordered drinks and toasted to Martin's health. They talked about the weather and nothing until the appetizers arrived, three orders of escargot, with all of the dainty eating and then the messy slurping.

Henri finished last. And right after he put down his fork, he looked at Martin and Michel and said, "Time to discuss the new realities."

He looked at their faces when he said it. Henri could not know what they were thinking. He could not know that Martin was surprisingly placid inside — grateful for his life and oddly unburdened. He could not know that Martin had embraced his notion. Better out than in.

And, as for Michel, Henri had never been able to read his younger cousin — other than his belief that, in Michel's case, the caricature told the essential truth: arrogant, ruthless, uncouth.

The waiter came to remove the plates and bowls and offered a second drink without asking.

Henri looked at Michel. He looked — no, stared — and said, "Martin owes his life to me. And you owe your continued place in this family to Martin."

Michel looked at Martin. It was an unmistakable look, a what-the-fuck look. He could not know that, in Michel's head, it was a what-the-fuck-you-idiot look — but the you-idiot part was often understood when it came to Martin.

Henri paused, sipped. Again, he locked eyes with Michel.

"Yes, he told me, you fucking scumbag," Henri said. "And you know what? I'll keep your secret from Gerard. I'll save your miserable fucking life. And I'll also keep the envelope that you give to Martin every three months."

Michel let all of that sink in. He looked at Martin again and saw a face that was... placid. But then he turned back to Henri, and Henri continued to stare him down. Michel seemed about to say something but then stopped.

Now came the trickiest part. This was the bit that he and Sylvie disagreed about. Because, on the one hand, Henri was convinced that Michel had set up Martin to be killed — and he now understood why. He felt he needed Michel to know that he knew, just to establish exactly where things stood between them. At the same time, though, he didn't want Michel to admit anything — because that would mean Michel would have to be killed, and regardless of how much he hated him, Henri did not want Michel dead. He wanted Michel neutered, not gone — because money was money, after all.

And then, there was Martin. Sylvie said, "He's an idiot but he isn't brain-dead. If you lay it on too thick, and he comes to understand what Michel was really up to..."

"He's closer to brain-dead than not — and this whole thing has wiped him out," Henri said. "It's a small risk."

Eyes still locked with Michel, he said, "How did the Garreaus know you had a guy named Ronny?"

"I have no fucking idea."

"None?"

"I've done some work in the 6th, hired some men from the 6th. I'm guessing, though. I really have no idea."

"And where is Ronny now?"

"I have no fucking idea — can't find him," Michel said. Of course, when he got word that the whole thing had blown up so spectacularly, the first thing he did was arrange for Ronny to take a premature dirt nap. The driver who met him on the other end, at the train station in Marseille, took care of that. Ronny's body had been tied in chains and was at the bottom of the sea.

"So, whatever," Henri said. "They turned your guy, right? They turned this Ronny?"

"We don't know that."

"Fuck you, we don't know that," Henri said.

Michel looked concerned, but Henri and Martin couldn't know that he was comfortable enough with the direction of the conversation. Pleased, even. He was fine with Henri thinking that one of his guys was a traitor. Better than the alternative.

"Look—"

"Look yourself," Henri said. And then he turned directly toward Michel — and actually shifted his torso a few degrees — and attempted to change the story his face was telling. His original goal was to convey anger. The change was more to show that he saw through Michel — a tilt of his head, a small roll of his eyes. He didn't think Martin noticed but he was pretty sure that Michel did.

"So, from now on, every three months, you give the envelope to Martin, and Martin gives the envelope to me — or we all fucking go and see Gerard in the Van Gogh room. Or, more likely, I have you killed first and bring the body and your story to Gerard in the Van Gogh room. The mess on the carpets, well, fuck it. However it goes, you end up dead either way. Got it?"

Again, Michel started to say something — about the money he brought into the La Rue family, and how the money insulated him. Again, though, he stopped.

"If you owe Martin, and Martin owes me, then you owe me," Henri said. "It's the transitive property of weasels."

44

J ust after 5 p.m., Father Lemieux emerged from the chancery and turned right. He went right, right again after a few blocks, and then left. Guy could tell that they were heading in the direction of Place des Vosges. He'd had four red wines at the café, and had bought another newspaper from a passing kid, just in case. And when Lemieux indeed stopped at a bench in Place des Vosges, Guy ended up walking behind him as he sat, behind him and then about halfway around the square. He could still see Lemieux from the bench he eventually chose, and he was fairly confident that between the spray of the fountain — two of the four were working, including this one — and the newspaper he was peering over, that Lemieux couldn't see him.

Ten minutes. Fifteen minutes. Lemieux just sat and seemed to enjoy the warmish evening. There were plenty of people on the streets — school kids rushing home for dinner, husbands carrying warm baguettes from which they'd eaten a bite, just the normal. And if Places des Vosges was a bit of an oasis amid the hubbub, the priest seemed to enjoy the calm.

And then he was up, on his feet and walking. This was

different than the walk from the top of the butte, though. These were not wide boulevards, not anymore. They were small streets, winding streets, narrow streets, some little more than alleys that could not accommodate a car moving in each direction.

So, Guy had to hustle. He almost ran to catch up to Lemieux from the other side of the square. At one point, as the priest made lefts and rights seemingly at random, Guy lost him. He reached an intersection and looked left and saw nobody. He looked right and saw only the hem of a coat that had made another right at the next street. Guy jogged to that next street and looked right, and he saw Lemieux knocking on a door and then entering.

It wasn't Lemieux's church apartment — he knew where the rectory was, and this wasn't it. Not knowing what to do, he found another café at the corner, and he had a half-decent view of the house that the priest had entered. He ordered another wine, and he sat, and watched — and what he saw was a fairly regular stream of men entering and exiting the house. All men. Maybe one every five minutes.

It didn't take a genius. Guy muttered to himself, "You dirty fucking dog," and then he walked over to the phone box just outside the row of café tables and called Timmy. The reason was simple. You wanted to know about radium, you called Marie Curie. You wanted to know about brothels in Paris, you called Timmy. If anybody would know, it would be him.

"Yeah, yeah, interesting place."

"You've been?"

"As part of my professional research."

"I bet. Interesting how?"

"It is professional research," Timmy said. "Trinity One is in a class by itself. To make sure it stays that way, I need to be aware of improvements by the competition."

"Whatever you say. Again, interesting how?"

"Interesting, like, well, pretty much anything is on offer."

"Meaning?"

"Well, you know how we have the costume room at Trinity One. Maids. Nurses. Schoolgirls. Nuns."

"Christ, nuns?"

"A first crush is a first crush," Timmy said. "I mean, whatever. Well, that place, it's not costumes, it's..."

"It's what?" Guy said.

"They'll piss on you. They'll beat the shit out of you. They'll yell at you, or make fun of you, or demean you. Like that."

"Sounds like fun."

"You should try it sometime."

"Don't tell me you—"

"You need to be open to new things, junior," Timmy said. "The little guy has a mind of his own sometimes, and he's curious, and you don't want him, well, you don't want him to starve from a lack of knowledge."

"Get the fuck out of here," Guy said, laughing, and then he hung up the phone and ordered another wine. After about an hour, Lemieux came out of the brothel and walked back in the direction of the rectory. Guy let him go. He had gained enough information for one day.

45

He had avoided the call-up for months, somehow, but then the notice came. Gerard had three days to get his ass to Metz, where his regiment was being assembled. The troop trains ran hourly, it seemed, in every direction. The telegram was his ticket, not that anybody looked at it. Nobody was getting on a troop train if they didn't have to. It wasn't like it was a damn vacation.

On his last night, Celeste decided to make him a picnic. They decided to enjoy it in the Luxembourg Gardens, and they ended up spending most of the night there. The place emptied out after twilight, but it wasn't completely empty. Every hundred yards or so, there were a couple of kids and a couple of blankets and, well, the night and the distance provided just enough cover. Gerard and Celeste made love twice under the stars that night, and ate a roast chicken, and drank two bottles of wine, and assured each other — not with words so much, but with hugs and hand-holds — that they would have a future together.

They both knew that her parents would be furious that they spent the entire night together, but, whatever. She wasn't a child anymore, and it was war. He drove back to her family's house at 6 a.m., and let her off a block away from the apartment just to avoid the scene.

They kissed in the car for several minutes, kissed and hugged, neither wanting to be the first one to let go. His train was in an hour, though, and they both knew it was time.

Celeste reached into the picnic hamper and gave him a small wrapped present, a book. He began to open it, but she said, "Later."

Then Celeste said, "When you read it, think of me. And when you finish it, know I will be waiting for you with a new volume."

After she walked away, Gerard undid the red ribbon and opened the wrapping paper. The book was The Red and the Black, by Stendhal. He looked inside on the fly leaf, and Celeste had written an inscription:

"For us, forever."

He wiped away a tear and then tossed the book into his duffel bag. The troop train was leaving in 50 minutes. He read the first few pages on the train before he fell asleep.

PART IX

46

On the first night back to work after his Lemieux field trip, Guy felt pretty well rested and more than a little bit excited. There was an opening now. He wasn't sure how to exploit it, but there was a crack. All he had to do was figure out how to bust it open.

The casino floor at Trinity One was hopping. It was Friday, often their best night. It was an invitation-only kind of place — you had to be recommended by a current member to gain admission — and it seemed as if a lot of the old regulars chose this night to get reacquainted with the craps table. They were two deep, hooting and hollering and drinking and leaving stacks of the cash on the table, bills that would be hoovered-up by the La Rue men wearing the tuxedos.

The poker players were quieter, as were the blackjack players and the roulette players. The craps table was off by itself, and a row of potted plants formed a subtle bit of separation. It didn't actually muffle the noise, not much anyway, but the impression it created was of isolation, at least a little bit. Not that anyone really minded the whoops after a big roll. Whoops were good. Whoops put everyone in a good mood.

Guy had been out on the floor for two hours, greeting the customers and accepting well-wishes for his father. They all knew Henri. They were all Henri's age, or older. Some of them said Guy looked like his father, which was complete bullshit. Others — usually, they were in the midst of seeing a credit extension — would talk about how proud Henri must have been.

All Guy could think was, "Yeah, he's so proud of me that he trusts me to bump off the family priest." That's not what he said, though. Mostly, he just smiled and upped their credit line by 10 percent. As Passy told him, "They're all good for it or they wouldn't have gotten through the door in the first place. The credit line is basically just a way to hide the gambling money from the wife."

Only when the request was for more than that did Guy say no. Because, as Passy also said, "The ass-kissing you receive is worth 10 percent. Anything more, kick it up to me."

Anyway, Guy was just getting done signing a new credit slip when the phone rang. It was Nico.

"We've got a problem," he said. Nico was pretty much running the skank place by himself at that point. Guy was providing very little supervision — he stopped in maybe once a week before heading to Trinity One — and the envelopes were just as fat as they'd been when Guy was in charge. He didn't know if Nico had figured out how to skim a little for himself and he didn't really care.

"Fat envelopes, fewer questions." That was another Passy-ism.

"So, what is it?" Guy said.

"A customer."

"Yeah?"

"He beat up one of the girls, drunk, just lost his fucking head."

"Okay. But, fuck. You know what to do when that happens. I told you."

"It's bad, though."

"How bad?"

"She's dead, bad," Nico said.

At that time of night, the drive from Trinity One to Boulevard de Clichy took about 10 minutes. When Guy walked into the skank place, the first thing he noticed was that the lobby was empty.

"I cleared 'em all out," Nico said.

Guy nodded and then said, "Where?"

"Him or her?"

"Her."

Nico walked Guy into one of the rooms in the back. He hadn't asked which girl was dead, but then he saw: Loretta. Guy had hired Loretta. She was just a kid from the streets, and he gave her some money for clothes and watched, over the months, as she gained some confidence and got herself a better apartment. He figured she was good for another year, not much more. She was talking about going to secretarial school.

And there she was, dead on the bed — her face bruised, her neck showing signs that she had been strangled. Guy couldn't stop looking at her, even as Nico tried to get him to leave the room. He just stared and got angrier and angrier.

The john who killed her was in the alley behind the brothel. Nico's guys — they were actually Guy's guys before they were Nico's guys — had already beaten the shit out of him. He was bleeding from a half-dozen places and his face looked like hamburger. A close look, and Guy determined that he might very well lose his right eye — that's how badly he had been battered.

The guy was in a heap on the ground, his dripping blood turning the cinders into a foul mud. Three of Nico's men surrounded him. One of the guys was zipping up — he had just pissed on the guy.

"Give me a minute," Guy said.

"But, Guy..." Nico said.

"A minute."

Nico and the others headed back inside. Guy walked over to the body — and he did think of it as a body, as if the guy was more dead than alive. He walked over, and he crouched down, and he slapped the guy in the face. His eyes opened, but they weren't really scared eyes that Guy was seeing. They were tired eyes. They were compliant eyes.

Guy leaned all the way down and whispered into the guy's ear, "A good girl, Loretta. Someone with dreams."

The guy continued to stare, seemingly at nothing. Guy got himself up and walked over to a barrel that was next to the adjoining building. On top of it were a claw hammer and a rusty saw. Guy chose the hammer. Within 30 seconds, his white shirt was somewhere between spattered and soaked in blood.

He took it up again, and then he dropped the hammer next to the body, and then he folded his arms and looked down at what he had done. His eyes went in and out of focus. Sometimes, he saw a sharp color photograph. Other times, he saw Dali. But he kept looking down. Maybe for a full minute, he looked down.

Then, after a single deep breath, he turned on his heel and walked out of the alley and back inside the brothel. Nico was waiting nervously, just inside the door. He might have heard, not that it mattered. Better if he had heard, actually. Better to know what he was getting into, what he had wrought when he showed up on Gerard's doorstep with that old letter. On his grandfather's doorstep.

Heard, didn't hear, whatever. He certainly saw the blood that was all over Guy's shirt.

"It goes like this," Guy said. "Down to the river — the boys will know where. Both of them."

"Both?"

"Both."

"Maybe she has family."

"Both," Guy said. "Both. Both wrapped in chains. Over the side at 3 a.m. The boys will show you."

Nico seemed frozen in place. Guy wasn't sure he had processed the instructions, so he repeated them and got Nico to nod in agreement. But he still didn't move, not until Guy put his arm around him and then gave him a gentle shove.

"The boys, tell them," Guy said.

Nico began walking.

"Wait."

Nico stopped.

"Do you have a clean shirt in the office?" Guy said.

After he changed, he got in the car and drove the 10 minutes, drove right back to work at Trinity One. He went back to the casino floor, and he didn't say anything to anybody, and nobody asked him any questions. He spent the rest of the night as he always did — counting the take, filling the safe, shaking hands with the customers, cheering their big rolls, lamenting their losses.

Only once in almost three hours did Guy excuse himself, and go into the office bathroom, and throw up. And when he thought about it, he realized that he wasn't sick because of what he had done — the guy was three-quarters dead anyway, and he deserved to be 100 percent dead. There wasn't any question about that. What made him sick was his certainty about that. What made him sick, Guy realized, was his total lack of regret.

47

W ait or sell?

Wait or sell?

It was the question Clarice was asking herself at least twice an hour, every waking hour. Her gain, if she pulled the trigger at the current price, would be 80 percent — and that was if she told Uncle Gerard and her father and the rest of them the truth. It wasn't as if the bourse committee on standards was auditing her trades and supplying a copy to her uncle. All he and the rest knew was that she was expected to deliver a 50 percent gain to the family on a quarterly basis. Above that, she received a bonus. But, well, really. She could tell them the truth, 80 percent, or she could tell them 60 percent and get a smaller bonus, or she could tell them 50 percent and put on an act like she just made it at the end. There was no way they could know.

She had decided on 57 percent — above expectations but not so far above as to cause a change in the current arrangement. If she sold that day, that afternoon, the La Rue family would get 57 percent (less her bonus), and Clarice would get 23 percent without their knowledge (plus her bonus). The family would get a profit of 2,850,000 francs, and she would get a profit (unbeknownst to them) of 1,150,000 francs. They would be thrilled, and she would be the wealthiest woman living in the shittiest apartment in Paris.

But, should she?

Wait or sell?

Wait or sell?

The money she was banking — from the original deal on the devaluation of the franc and from the healthy slice she was skimming from the family every quarter — had put her in a position to buy a seat of power, or close to it. There were companies where she wasn't that far away from being able to purchase a controlling interest, enterprises where she would call the shots and the little men in the dark suits would carry out her wishes. Middling-sized companies, yes, but real businesses with real profits and real decision-making and real potential for growth. And she could run them, and grow them, and sell them, and start again with something bigger.

It was what Clarice had dreamed about since she was 16. While other girls thought endlessly about snagging a husband, Clarice dreamed about buying a company — all while sleeping with most of the potential husbands, too. Because that was who she was, a person who took what she wanted, a person who did things on her terms. It was easy enough for her in school and in the bedroom — she scared off some men with her directness, but a lot more were more than happy to engage under her rules: no strings, no entanglements. The bedroom, easy. The boardroom, though, was different. There were few female role models there. The only women who ran companies were the widows of the original owners — which meant that, in most cases, the little men in the dark suits really made all the decisions.

And, of course, the place where she really wanted a seat at the table seemed the hardest of all. As long as Henri La Rue was her father and next-in-line to run the family, she didn't see how she could be given a piece of the action, a real percentage and a real say in the business. If Uncle Gerard lived long enough, she might have a chance — but, well, no. Because while he did sponsor her entry into the business, that was just about money. The seat at the table, that was different. That was family, and her father's voice was maybe the loudest one in the family, and, well, she didn't see it. Maybe if the old man lived 10 years — but what were the odds of that?

She looked at her watch. The bourse would be shutting down in a half-hour. She walked across the room to the ticker machine and began scanning the tape, gripping it between her thumb and the base of her index finger and pulling a six-inch length of it through. She would read that six inches, then pull another length, then scan, then pull another length, and repeat and repeat until she saw the ticker symbol RIO, for The Riom Mining Company. Pull, scan, pull, scan — she had become so feverish with the process in recent days that she had two different paper cuts on her thumb.

After about 30 seconds, she saw the RIO. If she sold before the close, the profit would be 81 percent.

Wait or sell?

Wait or sell?

She waited. And whether it was because of greed or because of fear, well, Clarice didn't know.

48

Killing the priest made no sense, Guy concluded. A victim of random violence — it could work, in theory. But given Lemieux's schedule, he was either with Gerard up the butte, or in the chancery with his staff or the cardinal, or in the rectory. His two-hour sojourn to the brothel was the only time he was really out and about and unaccounted for, but it was still early. There really wasn't much violent street crime in Paris, and almost none in that neighborhood, and especially not between 5 and 7 p.m., which was when Lemieux was out. Guy could hire someone to handle it, but the potential complications just weren't worth it. The streets and cafés were still full of people at that time of night. No, he thought, this would be much better.

It was Sunday night when Guy knocked on the door of the brothel near the Places des Vosges. The brute at the door let him in, and he walked over to the small desk where the man who collected the money and took the orders stood in his tuxedo.

"Good evening, sir. Have you been here before?"

"No, no," Guy said. "But your establishment comes highly recommended by a friend."

Guy leaned in and whispered Lemieux's name to the tuxedo. He was in the same business, after all, and he understood discretion — even if, in his case, at his brothels, most of the discretion involved lying to hysterical wives.

The tuxedo listened, nodded.

"His girl, well, he raves about her," Guy said. "I'm sorry that I forget her name but I was wondering... no, I guess, hoping... that she might be available."

The tuxedo opened his book, running his finger down the list like a maître d' searching for a reservation.

"Yes, Patrice is available now. Available only for 45 minutes, though, if that would be satisfactory."

It was satisfactory. The tuxedo took the money and led Guy back to the room that Patrice worked out of. Guy looked around as he walked, surveying with a professional eye. The carpet, the wallpaper, one or two of the girls who were waiting behind slightly opened doors. This was nicer than his middling place, not as nice as Trinity One.

Patrice was wearing a robe and a negligee. She walked across the small room, stood in front of Guy, grabbed his necktie, and yanked his face close to hers.

"And what brings your sorry ass to my room?" she said, her voice an aggressive whisper.

Guy reached into his pocket and removed a thick white envelope. She took it and looked inside. It was an inch thick and filled with 1,000 franc notes.

"What, is this some kind of joke?" she said.

"No joke. It's yours."

"There's nothing I'd be willing to do that would be worth that much money."

"You don't know that."

"I know. We have other girls for that — but, Christ, not for this kind of money."

"And that's only the down payment."

"There's nothing—"

"Just listen," Guy said. "Five minutes."

He sat down on the bed and she sat down next to him. The envelope sat between them. This was the riskiest part of Guy's plan. If he laid it out for her and she refused, or if she told Lemieux, the whole thing would be blown. At that point, Guy might have to hire a hit man or find a way to do it himself.

Still, he had a good feeling about it, and he just began talking. He told Patrice that not only was Lemieux a Catholic priest, but that he was the cardinal's right-hand man when it came to finances.

"I don't give a shit who he is," she said.

"Well, I do."

"You going to tell me why?"

"I am not," Guy said.

When she shrugged, he continued. The plan was simple: she would tell the fine journalists at *France-Soir* the story of the prominent Catholic priest whom she humiliated at a brothel on many Thursday nights. And for her trouble, Guy would give her that envelope and another envelope, just as thick.

"But I can't," she said. "I mean, this my job. I need to eat."

"I'll pay you as much as you'll make in the next year, just from the envelopes," Guy said. "And then the newspaper will pay you a second time, for your story and a few pictures."

"Pictures?"

"Front page, guaranteed," Guy said.

"But—"

"Think about it," he said. "It will be a lot of money, close to two years of what you've been making here."

"But I'd have to leave here, leave Paris. I can't do that. Paris is all I know."

"So you say," Guy said. "But think about it. I could fix it so that you wouldn't have to leave the city if you didn't want to. I can get you a new set of papers, and you can come work for me."

"Doing?"

"Same business as here. A nicer place than here, if I do say so myself."

Patrice sat on the end of the bed and stared at the blank wall opposite. Her hand had moved a few inches, Guy noticed. It was ever-so-slightly brushing against the envelope.

"Look," Guy said. "I know this is a bit of a shock but it's also an opportunity. A rare opportunity. You reacted so quickly — I can't leave Paris, I don't know anything else — and I get it. I really do get it. Paris is the only thing I know, too. I'm not sure how I would react to an offer like this."

"It's just—"

"I know, I know," Guy said. "So, I'll get you the new papers as part of the deal, either way. With a new identity, you can come work for me, and I'll be glad to have you. Or, you can just... go."

She actually shivered a bit when he said it, when he said "just... go." She kind of cinched the robe a little tighter and hugged herself.

"New papers, new identity, a bunch of money, and a new job if you want it. Or, all of that and a train ticket to... wherever."

She had stopped shivering. Hand at her side, it now rested fully on the envelope.

"How old are you?" Guy asked.

"Twenty-eight."

"I'm 26," he said. "And I know that I think about this sometimes. I mean, if I'm being really honest, I think about it a lot — like, all the time. You know how you kind of live in a box created by other people. Your family thinks this-and-that about you, and it's hard to break out of the opinions that they formed a long time ago. Your job requires this-and-that of your time, and it's sometimes impossible to find a way to live the life you want to live, or think about doing something different. You do things for your family, you do things for your job, and you never really do anything for yourself — and if you decided you wanted to make a change, to really do something for yourself, something just for you, just for your own happiness, well, you wouldn't even know where to start."

Patrice closed her eyes. She wiped a single tear, flicking at it with her pinky.

"I know you've thought about it," Guy said. "You wouldn't be human if you didn't. And, well, like I said, this envelope is yours just for listening to me. But if you agree, I'll make sure you have at least two years' money between me and the newspaper, plus the new identity, plus the train ticket, if that's how you want to play it."

He picked up the envelope, opened her hand, and laid it in her right palm.

And then, Guy looked into Patrice's eyes and said, "Haven't you ever wanted to just... go?"

49

I t was late Wednesday morning. Lemieux was already dreading the Thursday meeting with his staff, and then what he would have to tell the cardinal on Friday. The archdiocese was building a new school in Belleville, and the cost overruns on the construction were criminal, in the descriptive sense and maybe in the legal sense, too. The net result was that the archdiocese didn't have the money to complete the three-quarters-finished school. The cardinal was going to have a fit.

Lemieux had done a phone conference with the staff, just after having breakfast with Gerard. Dr. Benneville hadn't supplied him with the cyanide or the dosage yet, so the marmalade the old man was spooning onto his bread was as pure as the nuns who made it in their convent downtown. There was still time for that.

Gerard got up early and went to Mass at Sacré Coeur. After breakfast, he usually read in the reclining chair in his study. "Don Quixote," Lemieux noticed. Whatever.

The phone conference was beyond annoying. No one had a clue what to do about the school, or what to tell the cardinal. The contractor had been adamant — he would go to the cardinal himself if the payments weren't made, and there was no question about the work continuing in the interim. Because it wasn't continuing. There wasn't even a discussion.

After he hung up, the priest rubbed his temples. Then his mind jumped as if by reflex to the total in his safe deposit box. Two more years, he thought. There was plenty now, more than he ever believed he would have — more by a factor of five or 10 — but two more years and he could live forever like a prince. Maybe Casablanca. Maybe Marrakech.

He walked into the big sitting room, the one with the Van Gogh, and poured himself a glass of water from the pitcher on the sideboard. Silent Moe wasn't there — his wife had a doctor's appointment — and it was just him and Gerard. He drank the water, and the throbbing in his head began to subside. Two more years. Maybe 18 months.

Sitting there, he heard a soft knock on the front door. It was the newspaper delivery kid, and that tiny rap was his daily signal.

"The paper?" Gerard said. He was walking from the study toward the bathroom. It is what he did around 11 a.m. every day, after Mass and marmalade and then reading some novel or other.

"Yes, the paper."

"I'll be back soon."

Lemieux went to the door and picked up the copy of *France-Soir* that had been laid on the mat. He didn't really look at the headline — it was always screaming something — but the picture of the woman, well, it struck him for a second — but it was kind of like when you saw someone out of the usual context, like when you ran into the bakery guy at a football game. It took a beat before the tumblers fell into place.

And then Lemieux read the headline:

"SCANDAL AT THE CHANCERY"

And then he read the second headline:

"Cardinal's financial advisor frequents abusive prostitute"

And then, in dark type below that:

"If I had known he was a man of God, I never would have."

Lemieux looked over toward the bathroom, which was down a side hallway. He likely had about five minutes.

The big picture was of Patrice, and there were three more inside, one of them with her clutching a handkerchief and wiping her face. That was bad enough. At the bottom of the front page, though, was a smaller picture of the local pastor, the cardinal, and him. The three of them were digging into the earth with ceremonial silver shovels at the groundbreaking of the new school in Belleville.

Lemieux's hands were shaking but he was able to read enough of the story to know that he was cooked. He had no idea why Patrice would do this — for money, undoubtedly, but still. Did money mean that much to her that she would betray him? Did somebody else put her up to it? Was it Benneville? He was the only other person who knew about Lemieux and Patrice — but, no. Lemieux had as much on Benneville as Benneville had on him. Besides, there were the envelopes.

All of these thoughts flew through Lemieux's head, but then a noise stopped them. The flushing toilet, and then the taps on the sink being turned on. Gerard would be out in 30 seconds, no more. Not two years anymore. Not 18 months.

Could he brazen his way through it? Talk his way out of it? Tell Gerard he was the victim of a malicious campaign to discredit the cardinal somehow? No. Because even if he could snow the old man, there was still the cardinal and the rest of the chancery. They were likely opening their copies of *France-Soir* at about the same time Lemieux did. No. No.

If he'd had more time to think, maybe Lemieux would have reached a different conclusion. But he didn't have time. So dropped the newspaper on the table and hurried out the door of Gerard's apartment. He did take his briefcase but not his overnight bag or anything else.

Out the door, past Sacré Coeur, down the butte, down the steps, down, down, down in a fast walk until he hailed a taxi at the bottom of the hill. Right to the bank, into the safe deposit box, with an odd look from the teller who carried the keys on a huge ring. Maybe he'd seen the paper, or maybe Lemieux was imagining it. Either way, it didn't matter. He emptied the box into his briefcase — all of the cash, as well as his forged identity papers. He really liked the picture on the passport. In the taxi to the station, he silently practiced his new name, over and over. Claude Ransom. Claude Ransom. Claude Ransom.

There would be a train out of Montparnasse, he figured, a train south. It would have to be Spain for now. Not Morocco but Spain — just for now, though. He would need time, time to think. He had taken enough from his cut of the La Rue money to live for years, maybe decades. Not as a prince, but not as a pauper, either. Not in Morocco — well, maybe not — but certainly in Spain. Not forever but for years, maybe decades.

PART X

50

Business celebrations in the La Rue family tended to involve copious amounts of two commodities: alcohol and women. This one was no different, even if it was the first one attended by both Henri and Guy, by father and son.

Henri and Guy, Martin and Michel, Passy and Timmy, Freddy and Nico. Those were the eight. Nico had been a debate — Father Lemieux had been his grandfather's confidante, after all — but it was ultimately decided to include him. The clincher was what he had said to Guy the previous day: "That fucking priest. Thank God. I mean, he always looked at me cross-eyed, the fucking pervert."

Father and son, alcohol and women. This was a first — well, not the alcohol part. They had drunk together before, though infrequently. That night, the toasts by his father were as repetitive as they were heartfelt, and they went on until everyone in the room was slurring and stumbling. Guy had done well by his old man. He had done very, very well.

The women, though. Guy had known about the girlfriends for a decade — it was impossible to live in a family like the La

Rues and not know. But, well, knowing your father had a girl-friend was one thing, and watching him bury his face between two bare breasts on the next couch over was something else alto-gether. That was what was happening, though — and Guy had had enough to drink that he thought, fuck it, and got busy on his own couch, too.

They were in Trinity One, on the brothel floor. It was after closing time. It was just them, just the eight of them. It went without saying that the celebration would be kept secret from everyone else who worked in the La Rue family and especially from Gerard. It wasn't necessary to tell anybody, not even Nico, although Guy did say when the two of them walked in, "The old man can't know."

"Who I'm fucking? I don't tell him that."

"Not that," Guy said. "He can't know that I fucked him."

Nico nodded, smiled.

"I don't tell him who you're fucking, either," he said.

The celebration went in roughly this order: champagne, then the girls, then the food, then the brandy and cigars, then more of the brandy. It must have been 3:30 in the morning when Henri, knee-walking drunk at that point, sat next to Guy and put his arm around him.

"I can't tell you..." Henri said.

"If you kiss me, I'll fucking slug you."

At which point, Henri kissed his son on the cheek, and the two of them burst out laughing — piss-yourself laughing, maybe 30 seconds of it. Then Henri reached into his jacket pocket and took out the fattest white envelope Guy had ever seen — fat enough that the flap didn't quite reach. It was sealed with a strip of cellophane tape.

"You had expenses, I imagine," Henri said.

Guy looked at the first bill in the stack, the one that peeked out beneath the cellophane. Ten thousand francs. He looked at his father and told him what the operation had cost.

"That covers it times five — and it's still a bargain," Henri said.

What Henri did not know was that Guy had pretty much doubled the amount of his actual expenses in the telling — the money, the cost of the new identity, the first-class train ticket to San Sebastián. Because in the end, Patrice said, "You're right. I mean, who gets a chance to reinvent themselves? Not many. How can I not take it?"

Anyway, the reality was that his father's envelope was more like 10 times Guy's actual expenses, an absurd sum.

"It's too much," Guy said.

"Shut up — not another word. Like I said, it's a goddamned bargain."

They talked some more, drank some more. Across the room, Timmy was telling a story about himself and two women, playing all three parts in a raucous recreation of the events. Nico was both catatonically drunk and rapt as he listened, if that was possible.

"Wait — I didn't tell you how it went down," Henri said. At which point, he began to recount what happened in Gerard's house on the day the headline appeared in *France-Soir*.

"He'd just come out of the shitter," Henri said. "He said he saw just the last bit of Lemieux heading out the door, and then the door closing behind him. He didn't think much of it, either way. It was a nice day, and maybe he was going for a walk. Anyway, Gerard said the newspaper was on the floor, next to his chair. He picked it up, and said he didn't make much of it in the beginning. He looked at the girl's face in the picture, not really the headline. It was only after he sat down that he looked at the story more closely. The last thing he remembered was seeing the picture at the bottom of the page, of Lemieux and the cardinal."

"The last thing?"

"He fainted."

"Christ, thank God he was sitting down."

"Could have made a real mess," Henri said. "Anyway, I got a lot of details from Moe — he came in an hour or so later and found Gerard in the chair."

"Three paragraphs of detail — must have been more than Moe had said in the last month."

"Tell me about it. Anyway, your great uncle, apparently he's devastated. Like, barely talking."

"Must make for a bunch of long afternoons between him and Silent Moe," Guy said, and then the two of them shared another fit of piss-yourself laughter.

Before the end of the night, both Martin and Michel had also brought an envelope for Guy — not like his father's, but still. He tried to refuse — well, tried to appear to refuse — and they both said pretty much the same thing: "If you only fucking knew, you'd understand."

Of course, he did know that Lemieux had been taking a cut from their money — even if Martin and Michel didn't know that he did. He knew the service he had performed for the three of them by chasing Lemieux out of Paris. He knew that he had crossed a family threshold that day, too. His place in the family had been growing more prominent anyway, but now it was bigger. The celebration had been in his honor — his fucking party, his honor. It hadn't been two years before that he had been viewed pretty much universally within the family as a no-account slapdick who was destined to fuck up everything he touched. Now, this.

And if the envelopes were the tangible evidence of his ascension, there was the other bit of symbolism that always seemed to carry even more meaning for him. Because when he looked back on the night, and on his elevation in the La Rue family hierarchy, it wasn't the money that Guy thought of — or the hangover, which lasted a full day. Instead, it was the memory of him and his father getting lap dances on adjacent couches on the third floor of Trinity One.

51

It was two days after Guy's party, also known as the day after the hangover. Nico was sitting in Gerard's dining room. He'd been invited for lunch and was ravenous. At one point, the old man said, "Slow the hell down, grandson. It's not like there's anybody else here to eat it."

Gerard pointed at the platter. There were enough slices of roast pork and roasted potatoes to feed three more.

"Force of habit," Nico said. "There were times, growing up, when I felt like if I didn't eat fast, I wouldn't eat at all."

"You competed with your father for food?"

"I guess not. No. I mean, no. It was just that, well, we didn't always have a lot — never starving, not at all, but not like this. It just became a habit."

Not like this. Gerard smiled. If it wasn't the first smile in a week, it was in the first handful.

The newspapers had done their best to track down Jean Lemieux but without success. *France-Soir* had somehow managed to get a photograph of his room in the rectory, and it was pretty much a cell — tiny, with a single bed and a little writing desk and a prie-dieu. Gerard thought about Lemieux, kneeling there, praying for forgiveness from the God who would forgive anything, even the whore who whipped his bare ass in the bordello over by Places des Vosges.

Gerard shuddered. The man had taken him to Lourdes, had convinced him that faith could cure him, had traveled with him and prayed with him and taken the waters with him — and it had worked. Gerard was stronger, better, more fit than he'd been in years. But how? How could such a fundamentally flawed person have shepherded Gerard from where he had been to where he was today?

He shuddered again, and then he looked at his grandson shoveling another helping onto his plate. And then Gerard remembered at least one other smile he'd had since Lemieux abandoned him — a smile and a little laugh, actually. It was when he saw the short story on one of the inside pages of the newspaper, the one in which the bordello owner was quoted as saying, "Patrice is gone, but business is booming. All I can say is, the Lord works in mysterious ways."

Nico, meanwhile, ate non-stop for another five minutes. It was when he belched that Gerard jumped in and said, "I have a proposition for you."

"What's that?"

"I'd like you to move in with me. Plenty of room. You'd have your choice of two rooms up on my floor, or the smaller room behind the kitchen. More privacy, that one."

"I don't know, grand—"

"Come and go as you please," Gerard said. "Women, fine. I was young once. I'd probably draw the line at throwing parties, but other than that, no rules. And, as we both know, you already like the cooking. And you'd save the rent."

"I don't know — I mean, the hours I keep," Nico said.

"Meaning?"

"I'd never even see you. I sleep till one, out the door by three.

That's when you're napping, am I right? There's no—"

"I would like it," Gerard said.

Nico danced for 10 more minutes. The last thing he wanted was to live with Gerard. For the first time in his life, Nico felt like he was, well, living. He was worried that any change in circumstances — and moving house to live with his grandfather was not a small change — might upset what he had begun to build as far as a lifestyle.

Ten minutes, back and forth. Finally, Gerard said, "Well, at least think about it. Open mind, yes? Give it some time, some thought. Can I at least get you to agree to that?"

Nico said he would think about it. After two slices of lemon cake, he left for work. Gerard was a realist, but he thought there was a chance Nico would agree to move in. He hoped it would be voluntary. He knew he could force Nico, order him, but he didn't want to go there — not yet, anyway.

He picked at his own cake and then walked back toward the kitchen — to a room just off of the back, a room that was partly a pantry and partly for regular storage. There was a mountain of stuff piled against one wall, a stack of luggage and boxes that was more than a little unstable. He perused the pile, up and down. It took him a minute to spot what he was looking for and close to five minutes to secure it after unstacking and then restacking the pile.

It was a shoe box from Miller's. The logo was almost completely faded off of the cardboard. Miller's had probably gone out of business in 1930, Gerard reckoned. He blew softly and a small cloud of dust filled the air. He watched the mites fall through a shaft of sunlight, and then he carried the box out to the drawing room.

He sat down, with the box on his lap, and lifted the lid. When had been the last time? Ten years ago? Fifteen?

From inside, he pulled out a stack of letters that were tied together by a blue ribbon. He undid the ribbon and opened the first one. He had resisted doing it before, and he didn't know why he was doing it now, but with the letter in his left hand, he opened the drawer of the table next to his chair and took out another letter, the one that Nico had brought with him from Lyon.

He held them up together, one in each hand.

He lifted them up in front of his face and compared the handwriting.

It was the same. Of course, it was the same.

He put Nico's letter away and read from the other one:

My dearest Gerard,

I have no idea where you and your regiment are. The papers have suggested Verdun, but it all seems a little vague.

I worry for you, my love, and I will not pretend otherwise. But at the same time, I am filled with faith and confidence in your healthy return to me. We have so much to do together, so much to say to each other, that I am sure you will be back. No God would be so vengeful, no fates would be so cruel, to stop us before we've really gotten started.

The old man began to cry. He put the letter back into its envelope and retied the blue ribbon around the stack. Also inside the shoebox was a book, and now he took that out. The brown leather cover was nicked and battered, and the title was worn off of the spine. But Gerard knew it was the copy of *The Red and the Black* Celeste gave him after that last night in the Luxembourg Gardens.

He looked at the inscription she had written on the fly leaf:

"For us, forever."

It brought a tear the first time he read it, he remembered, and it did again more than four decades later. For us, forever. That was what Nico represented — the line, the continuation, the link with what was, with Celeste, with the only love of Gerard's life.

52

She now had a plaster on the base of her index finger and another on her thumb. It was the only way, at that point, to keep the paper cuts from getting infected. She'd had half of her breakfast and didn't even bother with lunch. She just stood in her office, stood at the ticker machine, and pulled the tape through her fingers — through the plasters — six inches at a time. Pull, scan; pull, scan.

RIO was up four points.

Four points since the open.

The price was 28.

The profit on the La Rue position was now 115 percent.

The reason her breakfast had been half-eaten was because it was precisely midway — one piece of bread eaten; egg untouched — when she turned the page of the newspaper and saw Robby Laperriere's latest column — and then she was too nervous to finish her food.

In the column, Laperriere mentioned The Riom Mining Company again. No sex necessary this time; no quim, no quid, no quo. Perhaps Laperriere had bought a position on the side and was goosing it, just because. It was unethical, and it could theoretically get him fired, but who was to know? He didn't even need to buy it himself, after all. He must have had a friend or relative.

It was in the middle of the column this time, the item above the dot-dot-dots.

The suddenly-sexy Riom Mining Company (ticker: RIO) continues to roar. A company known for its quiet trading and its consistent dividend has been roaring in recent weeks, doubling in price for no apparent reason and tripling its daily volume.

Traders, speaking in confidence, admit to being mystified by the move. A call to the company was greeted by this prepared statement: "The Riom Mining Company is pleased to say that nothing about its current operations has changed. Our belief is that investing styles go in and out of favor, often changing with the seasons, but solid financial performance and consistent dividend payouts never do."

When a reporter read that statement to a broker, he replied with an unspellable noise of disbelief, and then he said, "Current operations. That's the quote. Current operations. Nothing about the future. Seems a bit cute to me, a bit cagey."

That was how it ended.

And RIO opened up four points.

She had made the decision to sell when she was getting dressed. She would let the market open, let the stock run some more on the item, let the lunchtime crowd get their calls in to their brokers after reading it. And then, sometime after 1 p.m., she would bail.

After the lunch that she did not eat, Clarice never left the ticker machine. Her yanking of the tape through her fingers was so violent that she tore it twice.

At 1:15, with the stock up another two points, she sold her entire position. All of it, in chunks big enough to choke a horse. Her friends, both inside and outside the bourse helped her do the trades — and when they saw what was happening, they likely sold their personal stakes, too. But it was so late in the day that, even if they had wanted to — and some did — it was impossible to get their clients on the phone, to get their authorizations, and to make the trades. The price was still rising when Clarice started selling her shares, but it was falling hard in the final minutes of the session. Clarice was done by then, of course. If she hadn't picked the top, she was within sight of it — and she would miss every bit of the next morning, a morning that defined the term "blood in the streets."

In all, after commissions, the La Rue position in The Riom Mining Company had earned a return of 121 percent.

PART XI

53

The difference between a celebration of Clarice's family business success and Guy's family business success was plain enough: no champagne, no cigars, no lap dances. In fact, it was just the four of them — Henri and Sylvie, Guy and Clarice, along with Sylvie's go-to celebration meal of roast beef, roasted potatoes, and asparagus, followed by an apricot tart from Schiller's.

Henri recognized the difference probably more than anybody. Clarice had been killing it quarter after quarter, delivering more than the massive increase she had promised, delivering it every time. She dealt directly with Gerard, and then Gerard delivered the next of her latest success to Henri, Martin and Michel — and while there was a lot of complimenting her financial acumen, no one suggested a group celebration. It was as if she and her skill were being taken for granted. It also was if the rest of them had no idea how to celebrate with a woman.

The truth was, Henri was evolving that way. He had been adamant that he would not allow Clarice into the family business, but after she wormed her way in through Gerard's patronage, he grew somewhere between impressed and astounded by her success. She was producing real money for them, real money on a quarterly basis. And while he knew her hands were not entirely clean, what she did was largely a mystery and she was still off in her own little silo. Her office and the bourse were miles away from the family office and from Montmartre, both literally and figuratively. He even liked that she lived in that shit-hole in the 5th. The distance worked for all of them. And with each month, the father grew more comfortable with his daughter's position in the family.

Clarice had no idea about Guy and Father Lemieux. Her interaction with Guy on the subject — "How about that damn perv?" — produced nothing but a laugh and a shrug from her brother, a laugh and a shrug and a repetition of his months-long theme: "Now Gerard's going to have to find somebody else to suck him off."

Sylvie knew, though, because Henri told her. And Guy knew that she knew because, when he arrived at the apartment, she whispered into his ear after they kissed, "Congratulations. You engineered a fitting end for that fraud."

The dinner was like the old days — when the kids were in the early teens, unencumbered by impending adulthood. The four of them, back then, were able to be funny and witty and a little bit caustic without causing any serious damage. That had grown increasingly impossible over the previous decade, especially the serious damage part. But this dinner, it was a throwback. Henri felt it, Sylvie felt it, they all did.

Guy had taken one bite of the tart when the phone rang. Sylvie answered, made a face, and held out the receiver. "Trinity One," she said.

Guy took it, listened, muttered "fuck" and then "give me 15 minutes." He hung up, leaned over the plate and picked up the rest of his slice and kissed his mother and sister.

"Bad?" Henri said.

"Just annoying."

"Can't it wait?" Clarice said.

"Business is business," Sylvie said. She took the slice from him and handed Guy the other half of the tart to take with him.

"Hey, I'm not that fat," Henri said.

"Give it time," Sylvie said.

They all laughed, and then Henri looked at his watch and said, "Oh, shit."

"What now?" Clarice said.

"Late train to Lyon."

"Lyon?"

"Just business, baby," Henri said.

After he took off, that left Clarice, Sylvie, and the bottle of cognac that Sylvie grabbed off of the sideboard. The two of them drank enough and laughed enough that Clarice felt comfortable heading into the most dangerous territory that separated mother and daughter. It was during a short silence, when the two of them stood and began taking the plates into the kitchen, when Clarice just blurted it out.

"I want recognition," she said.

Sylvie was scraping a plate into the garbage bag. She knew what Clarice meant without further explanation. It was at the root of their differing views about what it meant to be a powerful woman in the La Rue crime family.

Sylvie kept scraping, one plate, then another, and then she said, "You don't need recognition. You have something better."

"What's that?"

"Control."

"Control of what?"

"Control of your life."

"But not of the family," Clarice said. She had filled the sink with hot, soapy water by then. She would wash and her mother would dry.

"Control of the family?" Sylvie said. "You can't get that. But you have something better, I'm telling you. You have control of your life. What you do with the money, it's a mystery, and it's a profitable-enough mystery that they're all afraid to ask too many questions or bother you out of fear of fucking it up. And if I know you, it's enough of a mystery that you've been pocketing a lot more than they know."

Clarice smiled. Her mother smiled back.

"But I want to run the family some day," Clarice said.

"You have no idea what that even entails."

"I have an idea."

"You don't," Sylvie said. "You don't have the first clue. And you're an educated enough person, and a self-aware enough person, to know what you don't know."

"I know plenty," Clarice said. One thing she knew was that her father had managed the business where Sylvie's old boyfriend ended up being charged with securities fraud and on the front page of *France-Soir* in handcuffs. She was tempted to spit it out, too, to throw it in her mother's face. For some reason, though, she didn't.

"I know plenty," is what she said instead.

"Well, you don't," Sylvie said. "And besides, when exactly are you talking about? Control the family? When? After your father retires? That's not going to be tomorrow. And besides — what makes you think you'd get it over Guy."

"I bring in a lot more than Guy."

"But Guy has a better idea of the business overall, even at his age. And he already has your father's ear. And, another thing."

Sylvie thought about telling Clarice the story of Guy and Father Lemieux as a way of demonstrating an important bit of the foundation that her brother was building. But, for some reason, she kept it to herself.

"What? What other thing works in Guy's favor?" Clarice said.

"Guy has a dick."

"Times are changing, old lady."

"Maybe," Sylvie said. "Maybe. Maybe a little. But dicks still rule the world."

Sylvie went back out to the dining room and brought in the bottle of cognac and their glasses. They washed and dried and drank.

"There might be a time for you to make your move but it isn't today," Sylvie said. "Own your life instead. Own it for now, and run it for now. It's a better way to live."

"But it's so frustrating. I deserve a voice — or, maybe, more of a voice."

"And you might get one — but one whisper at a time. Your voice starts as a whisper. One whisper in your father's ear, then another, then another. And I'll be in the other ear, pleading your case."

Clarice was scrubbing the roast beef platter and nearly dropped it into the sink. She double-clutched to secure it, and her mother noticed.

"I know what you thought," Sylvie said.

"Because it was true. Because you told me."

It was their biggest argument, played out over the years in several acts, Clarice saying that it was time for a woman to have a seat at the table, Sylvie insisting that the real power was away from the table, behind the scenes.

"I did tell you, more than once, and it was true," Sylvie said. "I was against you in this. I was. And I'm still not 100 percent sure. But you've convinced me, I think. At least a little."

"I haven't said a word."

"You've convinced me with your actions."

"Holy shit," Clarice said. "So you can teach an..."

"You call me an 'old dog' and I'll take it all back," the mother said to the daughter.

54

If you looked at it on a map, you would see that the train station, Lyon Perrache, was on the last little finger of land between the two rivers, the Rhône and the Saône. It really did look like a finger, with a snaggly nail at the end. Henri stayed in a workaday business hotel across the street, a nothing-special place with a nothing-more-than-utilitarian room, the whole thing catering to the Henri's and their needs. In on the late train, out the next morning to the meeting, back on the train that night.

The private investigator wanted to meet Henri for lunch. The restaurant he chose was one of Lyon's authentic bouchons, a place called With the Three Pigs. Henri didn't know a lot about the city, and asked the front desk for directions. The kid working there said, "You don't want to walk."

"Why not? Dangerous?"

"Not dangerous. Mountainous. It's way the hell up in Croix-Rousse."

Henri took the advice, had another cup of coffee in the lobby, and called a taxi instead. The kid had been right, and

Henri could see it quickly. The drive took almost 20 minutes —
it would have taken an hour to walk — and it really was straight
uphill for the last 10 minutes. Henri had been to Lyon, but it had
probably been 20 years — and he'd never been to this part, to
Croix-Rousse. He would have been exhausted when he got
there.

The bouchon was as advertised. They love their bouchons in
Lyon — red checkered table cloths, pitchers of rough wine, and
lots of pork in all of its variations: cured, fried, roasted, and
more. At night, the meal was often a raucous affair with friends
seated at long tables. This was lunch, though, and it was quieter.
Henri was seated at a table for two. Only one of the long tables
was full — old men, six of them, convivial but not rowdy. Maybe
they would get louder after the second or third pitcher.

The private investigator came in, and there was that
awkward couple of seconds when the two of them tried to determine if they were who they thought they were. And then Henri
just waved and said, "Jean Luc," and the investigator came over
and sat down. He was carrying an accordion folder.

Jean Luc Gilbert looked the part: threadbare raincoat,
battered hat, stained necktie. Henri's first impression was that he
chose the bouchon because he knew Henri would be picking up
the check, and a free meal wasn't nothing in his life. They
ordered — fried pork tidbits of some sort as an appetizer, shaved
little rosettes of something that tasted like salami in between,
and then big, grotesque sausages fried in onions and whatnot,
with a side of potato salad, for the main course. Needless to say,
Gilbert ate every bit and then wiped the plate with his bread,
and Henri made a point of not getting too close to the flashing
cutlery.

He had paid the bill, and they were finishing their coffee,
when Henri said, "So?"

Gilbert said, "Follow me."

They walked down the street and then walked through a nondescript doorway in the middle of the block. It didn't appear to have any special markings, and it led into an interior courtyard of sorts among the apartment buildings. There were a couple of rickety chairs, and a planter containing more weeds than flowers, and a mural painted on one wall. Swans, of all things. On one side, there were stairs up, leading to every succeeding floor. In the far corner, there was a dark passageway — also unmarked — that led to stairs that went down. Twenty-five steps down — Henri counted — that ended at another doorway and another street.

"Traboules," Gilbert said.

"Tra-what?"

"Traboules. The way the story goes, they were dreamed up in the old days — centuries ago — so that the silk weavers could carry their fabric down to the river to be sold and shipped, to carry them without them getting wet in the rain."

"A story?" Henri said.

"Might be true. Might be a little true. But it seems to me, well, rain is rain, and you still had to walk on the uncovered streets, and building these things just for the silk weavers seems like a lot of work for, well, I don't know. I like the other idea better — that the traboules exist for people to keep secrets, to avoid prying eyes. Worried about a jealous husband? Get lost in a traboule. Chased by an overly-ambitious cop? Duck into a traboule."

"I like that one better, too," Henri said.

"And so did the Resistance during the war," Gilbert said. "The traboules saved, I don't know, maybe hundreds from the Gestapo. They could never quite figure it out."

The two of them exited one traboule, crossed the street, walked 100 feet to the left, and entered another: same kind of unmarked doorway, same interior courtyard, same steps down. They did the identical thing three more times and then they were at the bottom of the hill, maybe two blocks from the Saône. Gilbert pointed up to the top of the Croix-Rousse.

"See?" he said.

"Okay, I get it," Henri said. "But, well, why the history lesson?"

"No reason. We had to get down here anyway, so I figured, what the hell? Here," Gilbert said. He pointed to the right. "Just another block."

It was actually another three blocks. But in about five minutes, they stopped in front of a shoe store. It wasn't just closed for the day, but shuttered. In the front window, there were a couple of empty platforms where you could imagine a pair of shoes being displayed amid an array of rabbits with ribbons around their necks. Two of the three rabbits were knocked over. Easter sale, probably. In the back corner of the display area, there was a battered cardboard shoe box and a single brown loafer that was propped up on its side.

"So, that was it," Gilbert said.

"That was what?"

"You don't know the story?"

"Not really," Henri said. "A little, but not really. Let's pretend I know nothing. It will simplify matters, and it will only be pretending a little."

"Okay, fine," Gilbert said. "So, this shoe store, this is the place where your Nico says his father — Gerard, your cousin, the elder Gerard's son — worked and lived. And it's where Nico grew up. And it's what he inherited after his father — your cousin — died."

"And?"

"Nice story, but total bullshit," Gilbert said. "It's an interesting story — I had a lot of fun chasing it, untangling it. You see it's almost true in some ways, but it isn't — certainly not in any of the important details. It's a complicated story — many different threads. Like I said, a lot of fun to unravel."

"But bullshit?"

"Complicated, like I said, but bullshit," Gilbert said.

55

The street was quiet, but Gilbert asked Henri to keep watching for pedestrians while also shielding him while he picked the lock. He said, "I've already been in there twice. Not a worry."

They walked through the shoe store, and the empty stock room, and then made their way up the back stairs to the apartment. It, too, was empty except for one beaten-up dresser and a couple of rickety kitchen chairs. The two of them sat carefully.

"Okay, so the shoe store," Gilbert said. "That's the end of the story in many ways. Let's go back to the beginning."

"To the woman," Henri said.

"Right, right. The woman from Paris, the elder Gerard's girlfriend from before the war."

Henri nodded.

"There was a woman — that much seems to be true," Gilbert said. "Birth records, death records — it's all in here." He patted the accordion file he had been carrying. "You can read it on the train. It's all organized in chronological order."

"Okay, so..."

"The woman, Celeste Lemaire, is legit. She died of Spanish

flu in July of 1918. Three months earlier, she gave birth in the convent of Saint Paul. No father listed on the birth certificate. Baby boy. Name of Gerard. All true."

"So, well..."

"With me so far?"

"The woman was real, the baby was real. The baby Gerard. My cousin."

"Right."

"Do we know for 100 percent sure that your uncle was the father of the baby? No. But, for the sake of argument..."

"Okay, okay, got it," Henri said. "Go ahead."

"The sisters at St. Paul put the baby up for adoption," Gilbert said. "A family took him in almost immediately — about a year after they buried their own son, a baby, in childbirth. In their grief, well, the nuns gave these people, Mr. and Mrs. Maubert, an opportunity. The adoption papers are in there, in the file, you'll see. The Mauberts, after she lost the baby, it was a mess. She almost died with the baby, and they had to take her uterus. So, they couldn't have another one of their own, and they adopted Gerard. They owned this apartment and the shoe store down below."

The private investigator stood up and took a lap around the empty sitting room. There was enough dust on the floor that he made a circle of faint footprints.

"So, that's how it went," Gilbert said. "Loving family has someone to love. Orphan boy makes good. Nice story. Nice family. Nice little business. But then nice little Hitler came calling, and young Gerard was called up immediately, called up in the initial wave of recruits, and he died in the first week of the war. Outside Sedan. Age 22. The army papers are in there."

He patted the accordion file again.

"So Gerard's son, my cousin, has been dead since—"

"Dead since June of 1940."

Henri didn't know how to react. Part of him had hoped that Nico's entire story had been bullshit. This, though, was real. Gerard did have a son. Henri did have a cousin.

"With me? Need a minute? You can go for a piss back there — water's still turned on, for some reason."

Henri did just that. The taps rattled when he turned them on, but they produced enough water for him to splash his face. There were no towels, though, so he wiped his mug on his sleeve.

"Okay, so there's all of that," Gilbert said. "Dead right out of the starting gate. One of many, millions, but still tragic for the Mauberts, no doubt. We both lived it ourselves. We know. They lost their baby in childbirth, then they had their second chance with baby Gerard, then they didn't. But war, right? Fucking Hitler, right? So, they keep going.

"After the war, they hire a young man to help in the store, a man back from the war. That was 1944. He is their trusted employee, their only employee, and they grew close. They treated each other like family, supported each other — especially after the young man suffered a loss of his own. And so, when the Mauberts died — the two of them, just months apart in 1953 — they left their only employee, the young man who took the place of their adopted son, they left him the shoe store and the apartment up above. There was nobody else, right? And that's where the employee, now owner, a man named Marcel Tremaine, a widower who grew closer to his employers in his grief, lived with his son."

"A boy named Nico," Henri whispered.

"Yes, Nicolas."

Again, Henri was overwhelmed by a wave of, well, what? He wasn't sure. Because he now knew what he had hoped to find out — that Nico was not family, not Gerard's grandson. He should have been elated. It was why he had gotten Chrétien to contact a cop friend in Lyon, a cop friend who could recommend a private investigator. It was why the process had started, and it was a process that had led to the desired result.

Still, there was this... almost nausea. Not like when you're going to vomit, not exactly, but this deep ache in your gut. It was almost like when someone close died, except it wasn't that, not exactly. It was short of that, muffled a bit but in the same neighborhood.

Gilbert produced a flask from his breast pocket and handed it to Henri. He unscrewed the cap and took a swig — and while the coat might have been threadbare and the hat battered, the alcohol inside was more than acceptable. Henri stopped, took a deep breath, and then another long pull.

"Thanks," he said.

"I would have needed more than that," Gilbert said. And then, he took a drink of his own. "The rest, I'm assuming, you have already figured out," the private investigator said. "Or, rather, guessed, because all we can do at this point is guess."

"Forget about my guesses. What do you know?"

"Again, this is just a series of deductions," Gilbert said. "The key information is documented and not subject to challenge or conjecture. The kid is not your blood relative. He is not the elder Gerard's grandson. Like I said, that's rock solid. It's all in here."

He patted the accordion file again.

"With that, here are my deductions of the end of the story," Gilbert said. "First, though, one more fact. Marcel Tremaine, Nico's father, died in 1958. Cancer. The death certificate is in there, too. I think it's the last document."

Gilbert took another drink and offered the flask back to Henri. He emptied it.

"So, my guess is, once Marcel Tremaine died, Nico inherited the shoe store and the apartment," Gilbert said. "You have to believe that Nico found the original letter from the dying woman, Celeste Lemaire, to her infant son named Gerard some-where here in the house above the shoe store. He probably found a copy of the adoption papers with it. If the Mauberts were like normal parents, they probably talked about their son who died in the war, bragged about him. So, he wouldn't have been a secret to Nico. And with all of that, well, it wouldn't have been that hard for Nico to embroider the rest. Again, just a deduction on my part — but the puzzle pieces, they seem to fit together rather snugly."

Henri asked a couple of questions just to be thorough, but the answers provided nothing new. The facts were incontrovert-ible and the surmises made sense. Downstairs again, on the street in front of the display window with the single brown loafer, the private investigator gave Henri the accordion file, and Henri gave him a thick white envelope in return.

56

They were sitting at the dining room table in Gerard's house. The day after his return from Lyon, Henri had brought the accordion folder and the contents were spread out on the table.

Gerard's reaction was odd, right from the start. Henri expected that his uncle would be furious for launching the investigation into Nico's story behind his back, and he *was* furious — for about five seconds. He looked at Henri, and his face grew red immediately, and he spat out, "You ungrateful motherfucker," but that was it. That was all the outrage the old man could muster.

He really was old, an old seventy-something, and the illness that had been cured at Lourdes — whatever it had been, and whatever had happened with the magic waters — took something from him, something that wasn't coming back. Gerard's color was better, and he had more stamina, but an element was missing — the fire, the sharpness, the whole giving-a-shit that had always been an integral part of his personality. He was passive now. The truth was that fucking Jean Lemieux had served a purpose — boiling down arguments, giving Gerard simple and clear choices. The priest had been more than a companion — not worth all of that money, but still. Henri was honest enough to admit that, at least to himself.

Henri told his uncle the story, step by step. He told him, and then he opened the accordion file and laid out the documents, and then he told him a second time. And while he knew Gerard was hearing him, there was something else. His uncle heard him, but Henri didn't know if his uncle was truly getting it. He didn't know what Gerard thought about Nico because he was fixated on three particular documents: Celeste's death certificate, his son's birth certificate, and also the service record that explained young Gerard had been killed in action in June 1940 at Sedan.

Henri tried for a third time, retelling the end of the story — of how Nico's father was just a shoe clerk who became close to the Mauberts, and how they left him the shoe store in the end, and how Nico inherited it all when his father died in 1958, and how he must have found the letter Celeste had written to her infant son on the day before her death. That's when Nico decided to come to Paris and pretend to be Gerard's grandson.

Gerard looked at Henri when he explained it — this was the third go-round — and he nodded a couple of times. When Henri said, "I guess I have to give Nico credit for ingenuity — and balls," Gerard seemed to hear that, too. He nodded again, nodded and smiled for just a second.

But as soon as Henri stopped talking, the old man went back to the three documents, especially the third one. And with his finger pointing at a part of the army service record, he said, "My boy, he was a war hero."

There were decisions to be made, but Gerard seemed in no position to make them. He was in this fog, a more glorious fog than Henri had ever imagined. His son. He really, truly had had a son. It was all there in the paperwork, in the birth certificate, in the army service record. Flesh and blood. An heir, however briefly. A war hero.

But while all of that was true, there was another matter. There was Nico. And while Henri was prepared to allow the old man his nostalgic miasma — hell, he had felt something inside when he found out there really had been a baby, that there really had been a cousin whom he had never met — the Nico business was a much more pressing matter.

To be fair, it wasn't pressing like with a hard deadline because the current situation could go on indefinitely, as long as Nico didn't become aware of what Henri's private investigator had unearthed. At the same time, every day that Nico was in Gerard's presence was a day that Gerard was in danger. Because the reality was, they knew nothing about Nico the person. From what Guy had told Henri, he was a good worker and a decent kid. Maybe he was happy in his new life and wasn't looking for much beyond what he had now — a job, some excitement, plenty of pussy. Maybe. But how could they know?

Because Nico was crafty, clearly. It took at least a little ingenuity to find Gerard and to recognize the possibilities. And if crafty Nico was angling for a big payoff, the quickest way for the reputed grandson of Gerard La Rue to receive that big payoff would be if gramps suddenly took up residence in a pine box.

Gerard had to be made to understand this — but the more they sat there with the contents of the accordion file spread out on the dining room table, the more Henri realized that this was not the day. Maybe in 24 hours, or 48. Maybe then the haze would lift and Gerard could be made to see the truth. In the end, Nico could be disarmed by sitting him at the same dining room table in front of the same files. It would be that simple — show him that they had figured him out and send him on his way. The knowledge in that file was a perfect suit of armor for Gerard — provided that Nico knew that they knew. The truth was, they wouldn't even have to send him away. The kid would run on his own.

So, 24 hours. Maybe 48. But not right now. When Henri stood up, he looked down at his uncle and saw the fog, and the frailty, but also a serenity on his face that bordered on joy.

He saw it, and then Gerard pointed at the service record again, and tapped it with his finger, and said, "My boy, he was a war hero."

PART XII

lara had made roast duck with cherry relish for lunch. Nico watched the old man tuck in and attack the breast with an unusual vigor. Nico was done with his breast first, though, and was working on one of the legs. The skin was almost burnt, rough in his mouth, crunchy and so good. That woman, he thought, could really cook.

"Quite good, yes?" Gerard said.

"As always, grandfather."

"I love a good duck."

"I love everything Clara pulls out of her oven," Nico said.

Nico licked his fingers and looked around the dining room. The furniture was not as delicate as the chairs in the sitting room, but it was clearly expensive. The chairs were covered in a blue-and-gold striped fabric that Nico was hesitant to fart on. His jacket was hanging on the back of his chair, and his sleeves were rolled up.

On the walls, well, they weren't the Van Gogh in the sitting room, but the paintings were lush and the gold frames were even lusher. My God, what had he stepped into? That was the question he asked himself whenever he set foot in Gerard's apartment at the top of the butte, and whenever Guy handed him a white envelope, and whenever he was diving into the latest girl that he and Guy had managed to wrangle. None of that had happened in Lyon, not close. My God, he thought. My God.

"So, how's work?" Gerard said. It was really the only question he asked every time they got together. It was the only thing that tied them together, Nico's employment in the La Rue family enterprise. From what he had noticed, employment was the only thing that really tied Guy and Henri together, too. Kind of fucked up, but, well, whatever.

Nico answered with a story about an overflowing toilet at the skank place, and a call to the plumber, and how the plumber needed a snake to clear the clog, a snake that snared the offending blockage: a rubber dildo bent in half like a V.

"You know, a dildo is..."

"Old, not dead," Gerard said.

"Well, I just—"

"Old, once young."

"Got it, gramps," Nico said.

Gerard smiled at that. Nico had been trying out "gramps" lately, and the old man seemed to enjoy it. He said it with a kind of cheeky edge that both of them liked. They were building a relationship from scratch, and that cheeky element was definitely a part of it.

Clara cleared, and Nico showered enough praise on the duck that she blushed. Dessert was a peach cobbler of sorts — just a mess in a baking dish, a delicious mess topped with a scoop of vanilla ice cream.

"Orgasmic," Nico said, when Clara came back with the coffee. She swatted him on the back of the head for his impertinence, but the smile on her face told a different story.

Christ, how long had it been? How long since his father died

— not even two years, Nico thought. The lawyer went through the will and told him he could sell the building for him, if that's what Nico wanted. And Nico said, "And what do you think you can get for a dog-ass shoe store and a beat-to-shit apartment?"

"About what you'd expect," the lawyer said.

He sold it, and Nico got half of what he had expected, half of nothing. It wasn't enough to start a new life, and that was what Nico had decided he needed. A new life. A fresh start. Out of that fucking shoe store. Out of fucking Lyon.

He was cleaning out the apartment when he found the box. He had known about the Mauberts' dead son, the war hero, but it wasn't like they talked about him all the time. Always in June, the anniversary of when he was killed, but that was it — and even then, Nico had been a kid for most of it and didn't remember the details. The Mauberts died when he was 15, after all.

But there it was in the box — the letter from this dying woman to her infant son, and the adoption papers. The Mauberts' dead son had been adopted. His original name had been Gerard Lemaire and he was the son of Gerard La Rue. He had been a soldier in the first war and he was from Paris. Gramps.

In the box, too, were a blue baby blanket and a postcard of Sacré Coeur that looked as if it had been hand-painted. The postcard was folded and creased now, but Nico carried it with him every day in his shirt pocket. Nothing was written on the back. It was just the picture. He felt for it reflexively several times a day.

One of Nico's friends in Lyon was the son of a newspaper reporter. When he had been around his friend's father, talking about stories he was investigating, the father spoke all the time about the "morgue." He said it was a library in the basement of the newspaper building, but not a regular library. It was a newspaper clipping library. Every day, librarians with razor blade knives did surgery on copies of the newspaper, cutting out every story — usually multiple copies of the same story — and filing them in different places. The same story could be filed under a topic (like, say, floods) or under a name (like, say, Jean Fourget, who died in a flood).

So, one day, Nico walked into the back door of the newspaper building — through the loading dock — and walked down the stairs to the basement. It was after the last deadline, after 2 a.m., and there was no librarian on duty, but Nico was able to figure out how the filing system worked after a few minutes. A whole wall of cabinets in the back was where the clippings were filed by name.

He went to the L's and thumbed through the folders until he found what he had been looking for:

LA RUE, GERARD

And that was when Nico found out that the man in the letter, the birth father of the war hero, was the head of a crime family based in Paris. He did the math, and the dates matched up closely enough. The rest was as easy as checking a Paris phone directory for the old man's address. That information, along with the letter from the birth mother to her infant son, was all Nico needed.

He looked at Gerard, who was looking at him.

"Gotta piss," Nico said. And then he asked Gerard to get him seconds of the cobbler if Clara returned with the baking dish.

58

Clara had, in fact, been back with the baking dish. Nico's face lit up when he returned, Gerard noticed. He dug into his second helping of cobbler and ice cream, and didn't take a breath until he was done scraping the last of the melted ice cream out of the bowl.

The spoon clanged on the china when he dropped it, and Nico said, "If I ate here every day, I'd be a blimp. I don't know how you do it."

"Self-discipline," Gerard said.

"Too young for that."

Nico slurped his coffee. The slurp was the only sound in the room. Gerard's plate was gone, and his hands were folded on the white linen table cloth, folded in front of him.

He stared at Nico.

He started, then cleared his throat.

"Were you ever going to tell me, Nico?"

"Tell you what?"

"Don't kid a kidder, son. Were you ever going to tell me?"

"I don't know what you're talking about."

Nico sensed something, something bad. He casually reached

behind him, to feel for the pistol in the side pocket of the jacket that was hanging on the back of his chair. He reached, and it wasn't there.

"Looking for this?" Gerard reached down into his lap and then raised his hand from beneath the table. It was holding the pistol.

Nico looked bewildered.

"While you were pissing," Gerard said.

"Gramps..."

"Enough with that."

"But—"

"Enough," Gerard said.

His voice was not raised, not by a decibel. For the next two or three minutes, the old man just talked. He told the story of an orphan who was adopted by a loving couple who owned a shoe store in Lyon. He told about how the baby grew up to be a young man, a young man whose life was cut short in June of 1940 by a German artillery shell at Sedan.

"You know this story?" Gerard said.

Nico looked down.

"The shoe store couple, they hired a man to be a clerk near the end of the war — a veteran like their adopted son," Gerard said. "They hired him, and they grew close to him. Their clerk had a son, Nicolas. Their clerk had a tragedy of his own, too, when his wife died. Do you even remember her?"

"I was three," Nico said. "I don't remember shit."

"A pity, that," Gerard said.

The old man looked at the young man's face and all he saw was defeat. It must have been a shock — riding a mountain of cobbler one minute, face-down in a pile of shit the next. Enjoying a new life and then exposed as a fraud. Poof. Gone. Gone like that.

And then, Gerard said it out loud: "Poof. Gone. Gone like that."

He said it and he snapped his fingers at the "like that," but Nico's eyes remained down.

Gerard reached down and picked up the accordion file from the floor. He pulled out his son's birth certificate and his army service record. He added a third piece of paper — Nico's own birth certificate — and placed them next to Nico's empty dish.

The kid gave them a glance that lingered for a few seconds — first over his own birth certificate but then on the service record.

"A war hero," Gerard said.

Nico did not react, and then he just looked down at his hands again.

"Here's the thing," Gerard said. "If you had come to me with the letter, and if you had told me the truth, and if you had asked for a job, I would have given you a job. Maybe not the same job, but a job. Maybe not the same pay, but a living. Maybe not Clara's lunch at this table, but still. A fresh start. You could have had a fresh start. Because I would have been grateful even without the subterfuge. A last letter from my beloved. News of my son — the first I had ever heard of him. Grateful, so grateful. I don't know how you couldn't have realized that. I don't get it. I mean, I just don't. You were the bearer of such joyful news. I don't understand why you felt the need to make up the story you made up. I don't know why you needed to lie, to pretend. I'll never... I'll never understand."

Gerard took a long breath. He felt his heart begin to race. He looked at Nico, and two different times, it appeared as if he was about to say something. Once, twice, and then nothing. The old man waited because, well, he did. He waited, and then it looked like Nico was finally going to say something.

RICHARD WAKE

Still staring at his hands, the kid said, "I just wanted to get out of that goddamned shoe store, old man."

And then he looked up at Gerard.

And then Gerard fired the pistol.

When he thought back on it, he wasn't sure if he actually heard the n-sound of "man," or if it was just the a-sound. Old man, yes. But some skills apparently survived the years and the decades. The single shot hit Nico just below his left eye. The body fell forward, and the scraped-clean cobbler dish flipped off of the side of the table and onto the floor. The china shattered in a half-dozen pieces. The blood from the wound threatened to stain the army service record, but Gerard scooped up the paperwork in time. He was clutching it when Silent Moe came rushing in.

That's what Moe said later on, that Gerard had the pistol in his right hand and the paperwork in his left hand — but that he was pretty much frozen in place, unmoving, just staring at Nico, at what he had done. He looked up and said, "Oh, Maurice," and then Silent Moe reached over and took the pistol from Gerard's hand.

"I'll call Henri," he said.

Gerard said nothing, didn't react. Two, three seconds. Then he nodded.

PART XIII

59

Henri and Sylvie at Maxim's.

A celebration, but not their anniversary.

They actually arrived separately. Henri sent the driver to pick up Sylvie from their apartment on the top of the butte, and he took a taxi from the uniform store. Sylvie arrived first and ordered a bottle of champagne. She was finishing her first glass when Henri walked in.

"Sorry I didn't wait."

He waved his hand dismissively.

"Traffic."

He poured his own glass, and she raised hers.

"My toast this time."

"Have at it."

"To a perfect plan," Sylvie said.

"A joint operation."

"And to perfect execution, which was all you."

They clinked glasses.

"Did he bring it?" Sylvie said.

Henri patted his breast pocket.

"All there," he said.

"My God, a perfect plan."

The "he" that Sylvie referenced was Martin. The "it" was the half of Michel's quarterly take that Martin was now required to collect and then deliver to Henri. But the money, while quite real, was only the half of it.

"Just think about six months ago," she said.

"Tell me about it."

"I mean—"

"I was fucked, or at least getting bent over."

"So to speak."

"It was the truth," Henri said. "It was all falling apart."

Six months earlier, Nico had arrived in Gerard's life — a grandson, a direct heir, a new presence who had the old man in his thrall. Nico's presence was unwelcome to Henri on the one hand and potentially disastrous on the other. There was no way to know how his weakened uncle might insist on playing it, no telling how quickly Gerard might have promoted Nico into a decision-making position in the family. But now Nico was gone.

They were both thinking about it, clearly, because Sylvie said without the topic having come up, "How do you think he is?"

"Gerard?"

She nodded.

"Pretty messed up, I think," Henri said. "He was already starting to fade, but... Christ. He fucking shot the kid for no reason."

"Well, not for no reason."

"Not for no reason — but it wasn't necessary. It wasn't close to necessary. We could have taken care of it with a conversation — just me and Guy, say, in the bar at Trinity One. Hell, I would have given him an envelope to disappear — and the fucking kid would have taken it. He would have understood the downside of staying around, and between what he'd made so far and what I gave him, he would've had enough for a fresh start somewhere else. You know, at least rent for a year and some time to figure it out. But then..."

Henri stopped.

"I wasn't sure the old man had it in him anymore," Sylvie said.

"I'll do you one better: I was positive he didn't have it in him anymore. I couldn't believe it when Silent Moe called me. Part of me still doesn't believe it. Of course, the other part of me saw Nico's brains oozing out onto the dining room table."

"How's Moe, by the way? He saw it, too."

"He's shook — which means he says even less than usual. Gerard wants him to move in, but Moe's wife is balking. The one thing he did tell me was that his wife would only consider it if Clara left. He said, 'She won't have another woman in her kitchen.' The problem there is she cooks like shit compared to Clara."

"Christ," Sylvie said. "Women."

They both burst out laughing, and then poured some more.

"We're going to miss that goddamned briefcase priest, just for the babysitting," she said.

"Speaking of the perfect plan."

"Devised and executed by your son."

"Our son."

"Our son," Sylvie said. "He's doing well — and not just that, I think. I can see it the way you talk about him now. Him and her, to be honest. Clarice is making her part look easy, it seems to me."

"I know, I know," Henri said. "I mean, it's... I guess I'm just grateful, which I know I don't say very often. Him and her."

"She's surpassed my expectations," Sylvie said. "She's a smart kid — and maybe not just book smart. You know what I mean? Maybe a little street smart, too."

"Maybe," Henri said. It was the first time he ever remembered Sylvie talking up their daughter.

"But really, six months ago — Nico on the doorstep, the priest nestled in Gerard's pocket—"

"And taking a shitload of money from the rest of our pockets—"

"And then, the great mystery of Martin and Michel."

"I know, I know," Henri said.

It was all true. There had been three separate challenges to Henri's eventual succession if and when Gerard bumped off. Nico might have gotten in the way, and the priest might have gotten in the way, and the combination of Martin and Michel might have gotten in the way. But now, all three threats had been disarmed.

"What's the saying?" Henri said. "That perfect planning prevents piss-poor performance."

"You just made that up."

"No, I read it somewhere."

"I like it, though," Sylvie said. Because she knew that she'd had an equal part in the planning. She knew it, and he knew it. What her husband did not know was how much money she had put away over the years, and how she was putting away twice as much since her staged blowup with the Chanel invoice, and how she was investing the money now, investing it by the envelope-full. Clarice told her that she couldn't believe how much.

60

Gerard, alone.

"Maurice," he called out, but there was no reply. It was almost 8 p.m., and Silent Moe had gone home to his wife. Clara had cleaned the kitchen and made up a plate for his lunch, and she was gone, too.

He was sitting in the chair that faced the Van Gogh. On the table next to him sat four pieces of paper — Celeste's death certificate, the letter she wrote her infant son, the birth certificate for baby Gerard, and the army service record. He picked them up and laid them in his lap. He didn't read them, not then. He just held them, feeling the sharpness of the paper against his thumb.

The little clock in the corner chimed. Eight chimes. Gerard couldn't remember what day it was. The newspaper was sitting on the table, and he picked it up. Thursday.

"Jean," he said, calling out. But Father Lemieux wasn't there, either. He hadn't been for weeks. He looked at the newspaper again, and then remembered. The headline on that day's copy of *France-Soir* had to do with an audit of the education ministry, and the headline said, "STEALING FROM OUR CHILDREN," but all Gerard could see was the headline from that other day, Lemieux's last day: "SCANDAL AT THE CHANCERY."

The house had been so quiet since then. It had only been a few weeks — maybe six or eight weeks — but the rooms had become like tombs, he felt. He heard every footstep he took. He heard every creak of the building settling. He heard every time one of the windows rattled in the wind. Sounds. Sounds in the silence.

He picked up the papers from his lap, and held them a little to his face, then he read. It was always in the same order. First, the letter from Celeste. Then, her death certificate. Then, Gerard's birth certificate. Then, finally, his army service record.

Gerard always lingered the longest there. It would be that way every night. He wondered, just for a second, if it would be for every night that he lived.

Gerard lingered even longer on that particular night. He caressed that final document, the service record, as if it were human. Then, he said to himself, aloud but to himself, "My son was a war hero."

The words hung there.

And then he called out for Nico.

And then he remembered.

————

I hope you enjoyed *Rivals*, the third book in my La Rue family crime thriller series. The rest of my work — historical fiction in two other series, both exploring the conflicts of mid-20th century Europe — can be ordered here:

https://www.amazon.com/s?k=richard+wake+books&crid= 1OV4YWKOCXPK

In addition, I'd love for you to sign up for my newsletter so that you can receive updates about future books in the La Rue family crime thriller series. If you sign up, you will receive a free novella that is a prequel to my first series. It features Alex Kovacs, an everyman who tries to do the right thing as the Nazis are preparing to invade his home in Austria in 1938 and ends up as a spy, and then in the French Resistance, and then as a spy again during the Cold War.

The title of the prequel that you will receive for free is *Ominous Austria*. To get it, just click here:

https://dl.bookfunnel.com/ur7seb8qeg

Printed in Great Britain
by Amazon